A Cousin Removed

Max Douglas murdered his wife on a pleasant Sunday afternoon in June. He killed her with the easy assurance he did everything else in life and had witnesses on hand to say her death was an accident. Chief Inspector Millson wasn't satisfied Daphne Douglas had drowned by accident. However, he could find no motive for her husband to kill her and turned aside to another case: the disappearance of a man called Boley thirty years earlier. His inquiries uncovered a grim and disturbing story.

Meantime, Max Douglas became involved with Poppy Latimer who worked in the florist's that had supplied flowers for his wife's funeral. But Poppy was not at all the kind of girl Max thought she was and when George Millson was confronted with another accident he knew that this time it was definitely murder.

MALCOLM FORSYTHE

A Cousin Removed

To Nancy & Sandy,
Love
Malcolm.

THE CRIME CLUB
An Imprint of HarperCollins *Publishers*

First published in Great Britain in 1992
by The Crime Club, an imprint of
HarperCollins Publishers, 77–85 Fulham Palace Road,
Hammersmith, London W6 8JB

9 8 7 6 5 4 3 2 1

Malcolm Forsythe asserts the moral right to be identified
as the author of this work.

A catalogue record for this book is
available from the British Library

ISBN 0 00 232412 1

Photoset in Linotron Baskerville by
Rowland Phototypesetting Ltd
Bury St Edmunds, Suffolk
Printed and bound in Great Britain by
HarperCollins Book Manufacturing, Glasgow

CHAPTER 1

Max Douglas murdered his wife on a pleasant Sunday afternoon in June. He killed her with the easy assurance he
did everything else in life. And he made sure there were
independent witnesses on hand to say her death was an
accident.

For the previous twelve months he'd been a model husband . . . charming, attentive and loving. It had taken him
those twelve months to regain Daphne's trust and confidence and to establish in everyone's mind that their marriage was a happy one.

The burgee on the flagpole at the Walton and Frinton
yacht club hung limply in the still air as Max Douglas and
his wife stepped from their silver-grey Volvo Estate in the
club car park. Max, just fifty, his dark hair greying at the
sides beneath his yachting-cap, wore a white short-sleeved
shirt and white shorts. His well-groomed wife, two years
younger, was in navy blue. Blonde hair peeped from
beneath a navy blue bob-cap and her plump figure was
encased in a navy blue T-shirt and navy blue trousers.

Carrying a picnic hamper and cold-box, the couple
boarded their motor-cruiser, *Moon Dancer*, moored in the
deepwater pool, her dark green hull reflecting in the still
water. The cruiser was the last word in comfort and fully-
equipped with conveniences like hot and cold running
water, a fridge and a television.

Max started the engines and cast off, his wife joining him
at the wheel as he guided *Moon Dancer* through the narrow
entrance to the yacht basin. Overhead, the sun shone from
a clear blue sky as the couple set off for a picnic on the
beach at Stone Point.

There was scarcely a ripple on the water as they glided

past the clubhouse and down through the moorings in Foundry Creek. Beyond the bend where the derelict hull of a Thames sailing barge squatted high up on the bank, Foundry Creek joined the Twizzle. Max eased the throttles forward and, with the tide at full ebb, the cruiser sped effortlessly along Walton Channel to reach Stone Point ten minutes later.

There were several craft anchored by the beach that was on one side of the narrow channel just before it opened into the sea at Stone Point, but Max took *Moon Dancer* to the opposite side of the channel, close in to the marshy bank of deserted Horsey Island where landing was forbidden. The Danforth anchor hit the water with a splash and there was a rattle of chain as the electric windlass paid out chain over the bow. Max waited until the cruiser was riding to her anchor, head to tide and parallel with the shore, then shut off the engines and stepped from the wheelhouse.

Beyond the low sandbank of Stone Point the cranes of Felixstowe Docks cut a jagged pattern in the skyline and inland the Naze Tower jutted skywards on the clifftop.

Daphne emerged behind him. 'Isn't it peaceful?' she said as a tern dived down, hit the water with a splash and soared away again with a fish in its mouth.

Max smiled and nodded. He went to the stern where an inflatable dinghy hung from the davits and lowered it into the water. Taking hold of the painter, he brought the dinghy round to the side of the cruiser facing Horsey Island where it was out of sight from the beach at Stone Point. He secured the inflatable by its bow and stern to cleats on the side deck, then unclipped the cruiser's guard rails and loaded the picnic things into it. He turned to Daphne.

'Ready?'

She nodded. He helped her down into the dinghy and as her trousered behind sank into the inflated centre seat, he stepped nimbly into the stern by the outboard motor and sat down facing her. He took a final look round. Everything was perfect, just as he'd planned.

'Is something the matter?' Daphne's round eyes were on him.

'No, my dear, I was just thinking what a wonderful day it is.' His blue eyes smiled warmly at her.

She smiled back. 'Shall I cast off?' Her hand reached up to unhitch the dinghy from the cleats.

'No, hang on.' The moment had come. Max bent his head and pretended to look down into the water between the inflatable and the cruiser. 'What's that, Daphne?'

'Where?' She glanced over the side.

'There.' He pointed beneath the cruiser. 'Something's caught round the prop. Can you see?'

She leaned over the side of the grey inflatable, her face inches from the water and peered into the gloom beneath the cruiser's hull.

'I can't see anything.'

They were Daphne Douglas's last words. Max leaned forward, took hold of her ankles and tipped her head first into the water. She was a heavy woman but she went in neatly, her body slithering over the side-tube of the inflatable like a seal's. He held on to her ankles so that she was face down in the water with her head and shoulders trapped beneath the hull of the cruiser. As she began threshing helplessly, he knelt on the plywood floor of the inflatable, keeping his grip, and waited for her to drown. Fifty yards away, on the other side of the cruiser, people laughed and frolicked on the beach.

Daphne's frantic movements began to weaken. Soon, they ceased altogether and the agitated water was smooth again. Max continued to crouch there, holding on to her for a while longer to make sure she was beyond hope of resuscitation. Then he released her and jumped into the water beside her body. Holding the head above water, he let the tide carry them round the stern of the cruiser.

As they emerged into view of the beach and the other boats, be began splashing and shouting frantically.

'Help! *Help!*'

On the nearest yacht two men leapt into a flat-bottomed dory, started the outboard and zoomed towards him.

'She slipped overboard getting into the inflatable,' Max gasped as they hauled Daphne's body and him into the dory and headed for the beach. 'I thought she'd come up straight away, but she didn't. I jumped in after her . . . couldn't find her at first . . . she—she must have gone right under the boat and . . .'

'Don't try and talk now, old man,' said one of the men. His companion stretched Daphne out face up on the bottom boards of the dory and lay down beside her. Tipping her head back, he pinched her nostrils with one hand and gripped her lower jaw with the other. Max watched in fascination as the man opened his mouth wide, took a deep breath and fastened his mouth over Daphne's. He blew into her lungs, lifted his mouth and watched Daphne's chest. He repeated the process four times in quick succession then released her head and placed his finger on the side of her neck.

'No pulse!' he shouted to the man at the tiller.

The dory grounded on the beach and the men jumped off. They lifted Daphne out and laid her on her back. One of them knelt astride her and, placing his hands one on top of the other on her lower breastbone, began rocking forward on straight arms. A small crowd gathered and someone wrapped a blanket round Max.

Taking turns, one applying heart compression, the other artificial respiration, the men persevered for a time before they gave up.

'I'm afraid it's no use, she's gone,' one of them told Max.

Max's blue eyes were tragic. 'I tried to save her,' he muttered brokenly.

'Of course you did. We saw you. You did all you could.'

They patted his shoulder sympathetically. 'She'd taken in too much water, though. There was nothing anyone could do.'

The dory, with Max Douglas and Daphne's blanket-covered body aboard, sped to Titchmarsh Marina where an ambulance and police car were waiting, summoned by ship-to-shore telephone from one of the yachts at Stone Point. The ambulance crew slapped an oxygen mask over Daphne's face and placed her on a stretcher. Loading her and Max into their vehicle, they raced away on a hopeless errand, siren wailing. The police car followed.

Later that afternoon, two watermen from Bedwell's boat-yard took a launch down to Stone Point and towed *Moon Dancer* back to the yacht basin.

At his holiday cottage in Duke's Green that evening, Max Douglas ran over the answers to the questions that would be asked at the inquest.

> *Why wasn't his wife wearing a lifejacket?* Because the shore was only fifty yards away, they were in a safe backwater and both of them were reasonable swimmers.
> *What were relations like between him and his wife?* Excellent. He loved his wife. They were happily married—lots of people would confirm this—and he was devastated by her death.
> *Were there any witnesses?* Yes, several. They'd seen him desperately struggling to save her.

Max mixed himself a large gin and tonic with ice and a slice of lemon and relaxed. He was rid of Daphne. And no one would be able to find a motive for him to kill her, however hard they tried. He was free. Life would be wonderful from now on.

Detective Chief Inspector George Millson gazed morosely out of his office window in Colchester. His bulk, straining the buttons of a grey, chalk-striped suit, overflowed his office chair as he sat with his long arms dangling over the sides to the floor. He disliked Monday mornings at the best of times and this Monday morning was worse than usual. Yesterday evening he'd had a phone call from his ex-wife.

'I want Dena back, George,' she'd told him.

Last summer, his twelve-year-old daughter had turned up with her suitcase and announced that she wasn't just spending a holiday with him as planned, she'd come for good if he'd have her. George Millson had been delighted.

At the time of the divorce, Jean had been given care and custody of Dena, Millson being granted access. With his unpredictable hours, access had proved a problem, though, particularly after his wife remarried and moved to Birmingham. He'd had to be content with infrequent, snatched visits that were unsatisfactory both to him and to his daughter.

His ex-wife had phoned the day after Dena joined him. 'She's only staying with you till the end of her school holiday, you know,' Jean said.

'That's not what she's told me,' he retorted. 'She's brought all her clothes and says she's come for good.'

'If she's not back here by the time school starts you'll be in trouble.'

'She doesn't want to live with you. She wants to live with me.'

'We'll see about that,' his ex-wife said.

Nothing happened, though, and after a phone call to her mother some weeks later, Dena told him, 'She's having a baby, Dad. She's not interested in me.'

Months had gone by. Then . . . last night . . . the phone call.

Millson stubbed out his cigarette and decided to walk up the road to the Red Lion for a drink. Several drinks, in fact. Running a hand over his close-cropped dark hair, he lumbered to his feet and made for the door.

In the next office Detective-Sergeant Scobie caught sight of Millson's movements through the glass partition and raised his head. Scobie, at twenty-eight, was ten years younger than Millson. He had striking copper-coloured hair and, unlike Millson, his navy blue suit fitted him neatly.

In the corridor Millson paused, torn between the instinct to hide his troubles and an urge to talk about them. The urge won and he put his head round Scobie's door.

'Fancy a drink, Norris?'

Scobie glanced at his watch. 'Bit early, isn't it?'

Millson grunted. 'Are you coming, or aren't you?'

Scobie's eyes flicked upwards. In two years of working with George Millson he'd learned to interpret his expression. Underneath that set face Millson was upset. Very upset.

George Millson had been a different man since his daughter came to live with him. Less irritable and easier to work with. Scobie hoped Millson's ex-wife wasn't making trouble.

'Coming,' he said promptly.

The report of Daphne Douglas's accidental drowning was on Scobie's desk when he returned from the Red Lion. Over beer and sandwiches, he'd listened sympathetically to Millson's troubles with his ex-wife, careful in his comments for fear of saying the wrong thing.

At the end Millson had said fiercely, 'Dammit, I wasn't the guilty party in the divorce! Nor was my daughter. Yet we're the ones being made to suffer. I'm going to fight this time, Norris. She's not disrupting my life again.'

Scobie read the report from the police at Walton-on-the-Naze and decided to inspect the scene of the accident for himself before taking statements from the two witnesses and Daphne Douglas's husband. Stone Point was only accessible by water and he arranged for the Essex police launch based at Harwich to pick him up at Titchmarsh Marina.

He arrived at Stone Point aboard *Alert* at about the time of the accident the previous afternoon. Unlike Sunday, however, only two boats—a catamaran and a cabin-cruiser—were anchored there today and there was no one on the beach. Standing on the foredeck, Scobie shaded his eyes against the sun and surveyed the scene as the helmsman held the launch stationary against the tide, her propellers turning slowly.

'Seems surprising a woman drowned here yesterday afternoon when there were people on the beach and plenty of boats in the vicinity,' he said.

'Accidents can happen very quickly,' the sergeant in charge of the launch told him. 'People don't realize how strongly the tide here runs on the ebb.' He took out a pocketbook, tore a page from it and screwed it up. 'Watch.' He dropped the ball of paper into the water. It sped away along the side of the launch and was soon lost to sight on the grey water. 'Tides are coming up to springs,' the sergeant went on. 'She'd have been carried away fast and it's almost impossible to swim against a spring ebb.'

'She wasn't carried away,' Scobie said. 'It seems she was trapped under the boat.'

The sergeant pursed his lips. 'Could happen. Depends how the boat was lying to her anchor and which side she went in.'

The launch returned Scobie to the Marina and he drove to Thorpe-le-Soken to interview one of the two men in the dory who'd plucked Max Douglas and his wife from the water.

'You didn't actually *see* Mrs Douglas fall into the water?' Scobie asked when the man had finished telling him what happened.

'No, the first we saw they were both in the water and he was supporting her head and shouting for help.'

The other man in the dory lived at Weeley. He was a

member of the yacht club's rescue team and trained in first aid.

'I started artificial respiration the minute we had her aboard and I thought we'd be able to save her,' he told Scobie. 'There was no sign of life in her, though. Not even a flicker. She must have taken in a lot of water before we got to her.' Like his companion, he hadn't actually seen Daphne Douglas fall into the water.

'Did anyone, do you think?' Scobie asked.

'Don't see how they could. It happened out of sight on the other side of the boat from the beach.'

Next morning Scobie reported to Millson that he wasn't altogether happy about the accident. 'It sounded straightforward at first, but after having a look at the place and speaking to the witnesses I think it's a bit—' he spread his hands in a gesture of doubt—'well, a bit "iffy". For one thing, no one apart from the husband saw her fall in. And for another, the men who pulled her out belong to the club rescue team. They're trained in artificial respiration and were surprised they couldn't resuscitate her after they'd pulled her out so quickly. They reckon she must have been under water for some time.'

'Do they now?' Millson's thick eyebrows came together in a frown.

'So I thought you might want to interview the husband yourself.'

Millson nodded. 'You're right. I do.'

CHAPTER 2

Max Douglas had been forty when he married Daphne. Until then he'd avoided a permanent attachment to any of his many girlfriends. As the milestone of his fortieth birthday came and went, however, he decided it was time to seek a wife. The decision coincided with meeting Daphne.

Daphne was thirty-eight and recently widowed. Very recently. A matter of days, in fact. Her husband, Peter, had been a distant cousin of Max and he met Daphne for the first time at his funeral. She was blonde, attractive and— importantly for Max Douglas—she was rich. Her husband had been a merchant banker. Max set about joining his future with hers; it proved to be quite easy.

Daphne's marriage had been a failure and she'd been on the point of starting divorce proceedings when her husband was killed in a car accident, saving her the trouble and leaving her extremely well-off.

Although Daphne had loved Peter when she married him, she learned to her cost that one-sided love in a marriage that has nothing else going for it is a bitter cup to drink from. She had no intention of repeating the experience. Next time she wanted a man who was a good lover and whom she could rely on. And she had no scruples over using her money as bait.

What appealed to her about Max Douglas, apart from his charm and good looks, was that he was quite open about his interest in her wealth. They discussed the question of marriage like a business contract. She would provide a comfortable home and the capital to set him up in a property business. He would handle her business affairs, be totally loyal and, he promised—eyeing her warmly—give satisfaction in the bedroom.

'I may require proof of that,' she murmured. Good-looking men were not necessarily good in bed, she'd been warned.

He smiled. 'But of course.'

He took her for a long weekend to his country cottage at Duke's Green in East Anglia which he'd inherited from his mother a long time ago. The weekend clinched matters for Daphne. Max Douglas was an even better lover than she'd hoped for. There remained two other points to settle.

'I don't want children,' she said.

He shrugged. 'Suits me.'

'And I keep full control of my money.'

'Agreed.'

They had married a month later.

'What do you know about this man Douglas?' Millson asked as he turned off the A120 on to the road to Duke's Green.

'Not a lot. When I called in the yacht club yesterday evening to take a long look at that cruiser, I had a word with the secretary. He seems to know Douglas quite well. Douglas has a house in London as well as this place at Duke's Green and he's well-off for money. He'd have to be. That cruiser alone would have set him back around a hundred thousand, I'd say.'

'Lucky for some,' Millson said sourly. 'And all you can afford is a sailing dinghy, eh Norris?'

'I *like* sailing. I wouldn't want a floating gin palace like that.'

'Nice place,' Millson observed as he turned into the driveway of Holly Cottage and saw the timber beams and the pargetting on the walls. Behind the tall Leylandii screening the cottage from the lane, the front garden was a mass of colour, dominated by red and yellow roses. On the concrete forecourt to the garage stood a silver-grey Volvo Estate.

'It's a bit isolated, though,' Scobie said. The last dwelling they'd passed had been a mile away down the road.

A sombre-faced Max Douglas in grey trousers and a navy blue Jaeger jacket answered the door. Millson noted the smooth face and unwrinkled skin of a man who carried his age well as Douglas ushered them into a timber-beamed lounge. Through a window, Millson glimpsed a gardener at work in the rear garden. He took in the inglenook fireplace, the latched door, the exposed beams and the wide heavy floorboards. An original Tudor cottage. Although he hated his post-war semi-detached rather less now that Dena had come to live in it with him, he still hankered after a place like this with character. There were some to be had in this part of the country, but they were beyond his pocket. Or if not, they were wrecks and would cost a fortune to renovate.

'Nice place you have here, Mr Douglas,' he commented.

'Thank you. It was in a bad state of repair when I inherited it and it took me a long time and a lot of money to make it like this,' Douglas told him. 'My wife and I only used it for weekends and holidays, of course.'

Millson didn't see that there was any 'of course' about it. If he owned a place like this he'd live in it all the time. He wouldn't want anywhere else.

The furniture in the room was antique and there was a bracket clock on the wall and a French carriage clock standing on the Georgian desk in an alcove. Outside in the hall a grandfather clock ticked ponderously.

Max Douglas indicated a buttonback armchair and Millson cautiously lowered himself on to it. He was wary of antique furniture. Once, as he put his weight against the back of a rosewood dining-chair, it had cracked. He'd been staggered at the cost of repairing it. Scobie sat down on a rush-seated elbow chair and Max Douglas settled into a bergère on the other side of the inglenook from Millson.

'My condolences on your wife's death, Mr Douglas,' Millson began.

'Thank you. It was a terrible shock. I still can't believe it.'

'Would you care to tell us what happened?'

'Yes, of course.'

Smoothly and without a falter, Max Douglas gave an account that tallied exactly with the one he'd given a police constable at the Marina immediately after the accident.

Millson's ear, attuned to Douglas's voice and listening carefully, could detect no false note.

'Daphne was stepping down over the side of the cruiser
into the inflatable,' Douglas explained. 'Here . . . let me
show you.' He rose and lifted down a framed photograph
hanging on the wall and handed it to Millson. 'That's our
motor-cruiser, *Moon Dancer*. The inflatable dinghy was lying
alongside like it is there. I unclipped the side guardrail—'
he pointed with his finger—'loaded the picnic things and
stepped into it. My wife followed me and somehow—
instead of putting her foot on the side of the inflatable—
she missed, lost her balance and went into the water.'

Millson studied the photograph. 'And where were you at
that moment?'

'Sitting in the stern of the inflatable about to start the
outboard.'

Millson frowned. 'So you had your back to her?'

Douglas hesitated briefly. 'Er . . . yes. Yes, I suppose I
did.'

'You didn't actually see her miss her footing?'

'No. But clearly that's what happened, else she wouldn't
have fallen into the water. It's all too easy to lose your
balance stepping down into an inflatable. They're fairly
unstable—not rigid like a conventional dinghy, you know.'

Millson shook his head. 'I hardly know one end of a boat
from the other. My sergeant here is the yachtsman.' He
waved a hand at Scobie. 'He knows about these things. So
your wife went into the water. Then what?'

'Unfortunately she fell between the side of the cruiser
and the dinghy and went right down under the hull. And
she didn't come up.'

'Could you see her under the water?' Millson asked.

Max Douglas shook his head mournfully. 'No, that's the
terrible thing. What with the shadow of the boat and the
murky water, I couldn't see a thing. I jumped in immediately, of course . . . dived again and again—' His voice

broke in a half-sob. 'It was no use, though.' He pulled out a handkerchief and blew his nose.

Millson inclined his head towards Scobie who'd been observing Douglas covertly, trying to assess the sincerity of his emotion. 'My sergeant has a question or two to ask. Like I said, he knows more about boats than I do.'

Scobie noticed a wary expression in Douglas's eyes as he opened his notebook. 'I wondered why you anchored on the Horsey Island side of the channel if you were proposing to land on the beach on the opposite side for a picnic.'

'Oh, boats often anchor that side of the fairway,' said Max Douglas. Though he'd made sure there weren't any there yesterday afternoon. 'It was crowded by the beach with all kinds of craft . . . yachts . . . cruisers . . . dinghies. If you put your hook down among that lot there's a good chance of a tangle when you come to pull it up. I've seen some real lash-ups happen like that.'

Scobie nodded. It sounded a good enough reason. 'I take it your wife wasn't wearing a lifejacket?'

'No. We're both reasonable swimmers and the shore was only fifty yards away. Now, of course . . . thinking back . . .' His voice tailed away and he shook his head sadly.

Scobie waited a moment, then said, 'The inflatable was in the water on the side of the cruiser nearest Horsey Island, I believe.'

'Yes, that's right.'

'I wondered why you did that instead of putting it on the side facing Stone Point, since that's where you were going ashore.'

Where it would have been in full view of the people on the beach, of course. Max Douglas had anticipated that question. 'Oh, because the lifelines unclip on that side. Which makes it easier to step over into the dinghy.'

Scobie, irritated by the smoothness of the answers and the confidence Douglas was displaying, tried another tack.

'I believe the tide was running strongly at the time?'

'Yes, it was at full ebb.'

'Yet it didn't carry your wife away from under the hull? Didn't carry her clear?'

Max Douglas appeared to consider the point. After a moment he said, 'I think we were slightly sideways on to the tide and she must have been trapped against the keel.'

'So how long would you estimate your wife was under the water?'

'Oh, I've no idea, Sergeant. It seemed an age to me, trying to locate her. But I really don't know.'

Scobie nodded to Millson. 'Those are all the questions I had.'

Millson had been watching Douglas closely as he answered Scobie. Douglas was cool and confident, not really distressed, despite the earlier display with the handkerchief. The moist eyes? Simply a crocodile tear or two. Millson had no compunction in putting his next question.

'Mr Douglas, don't misunderstand me, I have to ask this question. Were you and your wife on good terms?'

'Oh yes. We were very happy, Chief Inspector, very happy indeed. Ask anyone.'

The answer came out too readily for Millson's liking, especially the invitation to 'ask anyone'. Husbands didn't usually make a point of inviting you to check on their relationship with their wives.

'And to save you the embarrassment of asking, Chief Inspector,' Douglas went on, 'everything passes to me under my wife's will. She was very wealthy.' He looked Millson full in the face. 'And so am I,' he added.

The emphasis was not lost on Millson. Douglas meant: 'Just in case your nasty policeman's mind is thinking it wasn't an accident and I killed her for her money.'

Millson nodded and rose to his feet. 'Thank you for answering our questions, Mr Douglas. My condolences once more on your loss and I hope we shan't need to bother you again.'

'A cool customer, that one,' Millson said as they drove away. 'Didn't care for him at all. Handsome blighter, though. I'll bet he has no trouble pulling the girls.'

'Maybe involved with a girl and tired of his wife?' Scobie suggested. 'Shall I make some inquiries?'

'No, waste of time. When a husband tells you everyone will confirm he and his wife were very happy, you can reckon he's bulletproof on that. Same with the money. He's obviously rolling, like he says. What about his explanation of the accident? You're the sailor—what d'you think?'

'It was credible. An accident could happen like that.' Scobie shook his head doubtfully. 'But if it did, Daphne Douglas was a *very* unlucky woman.'

'Why d'you say that?'

Scobie ticked off the points on his fingers: 'One. They anchor on the other side of the fairway by Horsey Island where there's no one about. Two. The guardrails happen to unclip on the side of the boat nearest to Horsey Island so that she has to get into the inflatable out of sight of the people on the beach at Stone Point and the other boats. Three. She falls between the inflatable and the cruiser and goes underneath the hull. Four. The tide traps her there and holds her underwater long enough to drown.'

'So what are you saying, Norris? That he planned the whole thing? Pushed her in and held her under where no one could see?'

Scobie looked uncomfortable. 'It's possible,' he muttered.

'You need a motive for that. And we don't have one, because I think we can assume there isn't another woman and he didn't do it for money. He wasn't particularly upset by his wife's death, but that doesn't mean he murdered her. Not without a motive. Do you have one?'

Scobie shook his head. 'No, I just don't believe she could have been that unlucky.'

Millson drove for a time in silence. Then he said, 'Why do I have this feeling you may be right, Norris, and Douglas was conning us?'

'Because he was, perhaps?'

Millson grimaced. 'Jean used to say my problem is that I think everyone's a villain. She said I don't like people.'

'That's not true,' Scobie said. 'And from what you told me yesterday lunch-time, I wouldn't give a toss for your ex-wife's opinion.'

Millson grinned. 'Thanks for the loyalty, Norris. Let's get back to Douglas. If you're going to drown your wife, would you do it with dozens of people around?'

'I might do if I wanted to stage an accident.'

Millson thought for a while, considering the points Scobie had listed. Finally he shook his head. 'We have to let it go. There isn't enough to ask the coroner to adjourn the inquest.'

Max Douglas stood watching through the window as the two policemen drove away, running over their questions and his answers in his mind. He'd made no slip-ups and hadn't stumbled. Altogether a convincing performance, he thought, and the police had seemed satisfied Daphne's death was an accident. Anyway, they could make all the inquiries they liked. There was no evidence to show he'd murdered her and they'd never discover his reason for killing her.

He turned from the window and sat down in the bergère chair to replan his future, a future without Daphne.

Tomorrow, he would return to the London house and make arrangements for the funeral.

CHAPTER 3

The day of Daphne Douglas's funeral was bright, with cool sunshine, but the June weather had become unsettled and a thunderstorm was not far off.

The inquest three days ago had passed without incident and with no awkward questions. The coroner, after stressing the importance of wearing a lifejacket at all times on the water, had returned a verdict of accidental death.

As the time of the funeral approached that day, Max began to feel elated . . . keyed up. Not only because he was free, but because being alive in the presence of death provoked excitement in him . . . a sense of expectancy . . . a heightened awareness of life that was stimulating.

Funerals always had this effect on him. They reawakened the childhood trauma of an uncle's funeral many years ago. His uncle's family had been close-knit and loving and the emotional atmosphere at the house as Max's aunt and two teenaged cousins prepared to leave for the ceremony had been highly charged. He recalled vividly the eroticism of the uniform black skirts and dresses, the black stockings and tights. And the undertaker's men—satanic youths, black-gloved hands gripping the coffin—their eyes roaming over the crying females like victors surveying defenceless women whose man had died in battle.

At the graveside, the tension as the gleaming coffin entered the close-fitting grave had been unbearable. For nights afterwards in bed, the young Max imagined himself being slowly lowered into a grave with black skirts and dresses clustered around it giving glimpses of secret white flesh.

He'd been appalled when, after the ceremony, the mourners had suddenly been transformed into cheerful,

chatty survivors, scampering back to the deceased's house
to eat and drink greedily at the widow's expense. And he'd
been disturbed at the way the men hung round his aunt
and her attractive daughters, consoling them with an eager-
ness that was obscene.

He remembered he'd cried—he'd been nine or ten at the
time—and his aunt had comforted him, cuddling his head
to her bosom. To this day, he could still recapture the scent
of her perfume and her softness against his cheek.

In their house in Brentwood, Wilfred Mortimer and his
wife were preparing to leave for the funeral. Wilfred had
conflicting feelings about Daphne's death. He was sorry
about it, of course—forty-eight was no age to die—but he
couldn't avoid the selfish thought that he and Max could
now undertake the cruise they'd been planning on Max's
boat without worrying whether Daphne minded or not.

They'd have to allow a decent interval to elapse, of
course, Wilfred told himself as he searched the tie-rack
on his wardrobe door for a black tie. He had a black tie
somewhere. Then he remembered he'd put it away in a
suitcase with his black socks and other rarely-worn clothes
after a previous funeral. He lifted the suitcase down from
on top of the wardrobe and laid it on the bed, humming
cheerfully.

At the dressing-table his wife, Mavis, said severely, 'I
don't know what makes you so happy. We're going to a
funeral, not a wedding.'

'Sorry, dear.' Wilfred stopped humming.

The reason he was feeling cheerful was that Daphne's
death had brought much nearer the time when he could
escape from Mavis for a while. However, Mavis had been
fond of Daphne and this was not the moment to tell her
about his and Max's plans.

Mavis leaned forward and peered at herself in the mirror
to fiddle with a piece of black veil she'd attached to her hat.

'I'm glad Daphne's being buried and not cremated,' she said. 'Cremations are so cold and clinical. And they're over so quickly you hardly have time for a proper cry. Daphne told me she'd put it in her will, you know—about not being cremated, I mean.' Mavis's voice contained a note of satisfaction that she'd enjoyed Daphne's confidence on this point.

She sat back on her stool, turning her head from side to side to see if the veil hung straight. Satisfied, she patted her grey hair into place. 'And I'm not having you put *me* in the furnace when I die, Wilfred.'

'I wouldn't do that, dear.'

'I've put it in my will.'

'Put what, dear?'

'About being buried, of course.'

The prospect of Mavis dying before him hadn't arisen in Wilfred's mind before. He saw it now as a possibility. Distant, perhaps, but possible. A future escape for him, too.

When they arrived at Max's large Victorian house in Wimbledon to join the funeral procession, it was swarming with Daphne's and Max's relatives. The men were in the road jockeying their cars for position and arguing over who should precede whom and the women were milling about the house. Wilfred knew most of them—he'd been friends with Max for a long time—but there was a young blonde girl among them he hadn't seen before. Her black skirt was shorter than the others and her black tights had a zig-zag pattern on them. He wondered who she was.

At the church, the number of mourners swelled as they were joined by friends and neighbours. 'Daphne would have loved to see so many people here,' Mavis whispered, looking around and dabbing her eyes.

After the burial she lingered at the graveside, checking that their own wreath was among the flowers and wreaths arrayed there and looking at the cards and see who had sent which.

'What a shame Daphne can't see all these lovely flowers,' she said tearfully. She bent over a small spray of flowers and frowned at the name on the card attached to it. 'Poppy? Who on earth is Poppy?'

Back at the house again later, Wilfred noticed the blonde girl in the short skirt had removed her jacket and was helping with the drinks and food. The open neck of her white blouse revealed glimpses of a black bra as she moved about and he wondered idly if the rest of her underwear was black too. She looked out of place among the mourners and he asked Max who she was.

'H'm? Who, old chap?' Max ran a hand over his wavy greying hair that always looked as though it had been permed, but hadn't.

'The girl in the short skirt.'

Wilfred realized afterwards that he should have been alerted by the way Max made such a business of sweeping his eyes several times over the gathering of people before locating the conspicuous young blonde.

'Oh, *her*,' Max said, screwing up his eyes and studying the girl as though uncertain who she was. 'Um . . . oh, yes. That's Poppy Latimer. She's helping out. She's a distant relative of mine.' He gave a slight laugh. 'Poppy's a sort of third cousin twice removed, I believe.'

Third cousin twice removed or not, during the afternoon Wilfred intercepted some meaningful glances between Max and the girl and noticed they carefully avoided each other. That, too, should have aroused his suspicions. But Max Douglas was his oldest friend and it never crossed Wilfred's mind that Max would do anything underhand.

Wilfred had assumed the loss of his wife would make Max even keener on their planned holiday on his boat, because it would take his mind off her death. But he didn't like to tackle him about it too soon after the funeral and he decided to wait patiently for Max to bring up the subject himself.

Max did no such thing, however. A week after the funeral, Max Douglas put his London house and his business on the market, sold his boat and decamped to the Costa del Sol. With Poppy Latimer.

Wilfred was dumbfounded. There had been no warning, no hint, nothing.

Mavis was scandalized. 'The girl's young enough to be his daughter!'

Daughter? A few years younger and she could be his granddaughter, Wilfred thought. Max was the same age as he was.

'And his poor wife not yet cold in her grave,' Mavis added innacurately. Her mouth twisted unpleasantly. 'The girl's a gold-digger.'

Probably. Though Wilfred Mortimer wouldn't have minded Poppy Latimer digging for his gold, if he had any —which he hadn't. And even if he had, Poppy Latimer wouldn't have run off with him. He didn't have Max's charm. Max had a way with young girls. That warm, courteous smile, the distinguished greying hair and safe, fatherly manner had always drawn young girls to him like a magnet. Even Wilfred's own daughter had been smitten by his charm when she was a teenager.

'I could easily fall for Uncle Max,' Pamela used to say. 'He's such a pet.'

According to Mavis, Poppy Latimer had been working in the florist's where Max went to order the wreaths and flowers for Daphne's funeral. Poppy told him who she was —third cousin twice removed, or whatever—and attraction had been instant and mutual apparently. 'Lust at first sight,' Mavis called it. She'd prised the story from one of her contacts among Daphne's relatives.

'They've only known each other two minutes,' Mavis said with exaggeration. 'And they're related. *By blood*.' She rolled the two words round her tongue, like a wine-taster. 'It's incest. Incest!' she repeated with relish.

'She's a very *distant* relation,' Wilfred protested. Max's perfidy hadn't destroyed Wilfred's sense of fairness towards the man he'd been friends with for so long.

'*And* she's under age,' Mavis trumpeted. 'She's still at school!'

'*Drama* school,' Wilfred corrected. He'd made some inquiries of his own. 'She's eighteen.'

'Maybe,' said Mavis, 'but the family won't stand for that sort of thing, you know. They'll go after them and bring her back.'

Wilfred visualized a brigade of Daphne's relatives flying off to the Costa del Sol on Iberia airlines. They'd be armed with marriage and birth certificates and a copy of the family tree, intent on dragging an unwilling Poppy Latimer back by her hair. Somehow, he didn't think she'd come.

'I suppose you're jealous,' Mavis said accusingly, seeing his smile.

'No, of course not.'

He was, but not for the reason Mavis thought. He was jealous of Max's freedom. Wilfred longed to make his own escape from the dullness of a too long married life.

'She's a strumpet!' was Mavis's final verdict. He wondered where she'd picked up that label. Probably from Daphne's relative. It was certainly not a Mavis word.

There had been a brief, embarrassed goodbye from Max on the telephone. 'You only live once, old chap,' he'd mumbled apologetically. 'Fellow has to grab his chance when it comes.'

Wilfred winced as he thought of Max in sunny Spain. Max would be languishing on the hot sand in bathing trunks with the curvaceous Poppy in the briefest of bikinis dancing attendance on him. In the past, Wilfred had often seen girls—particularly young ones—falling over themselves to dance attendance on Max. He had that effect on them. He was a good-looking man and the years had been kind to him. Apart from the crowsfeet at the corners of his eyes, which gave him the appearance of always smiling, his face was smooth and unlined. It probably helped that he never worried . . . he wasn't the worrying type. Nor did Max have much of a conscience, Wilfred thought, which was probably the reason he'd been so successful in the property business.

Wilfred wondered whether Poppy would strip Max of what she could and move on quickly or suck him dry slowly, until he had nothing left. Perhaps neither. Perhaps she'd simply been looking for a safe, comfortable berth and would stick with Max through old age and infirmity to his death.

There had been something about the girl that didn't fit any of those scenarios, though, Wilfred thought. The way she dressed and the way she acted certainly warranted Mavis's description of her. But the expression in her eyes, when he'd caught a look from them, had given Wilfred the impression that Poppy Latimer was a very different girl from the one she was presenting to Max and the world.

CHAPTER 4

In the village of Tanniford, twenty miles away from Max Douglas's cottage in Duke's Green, Emily Boley puffed her way up the narrow staircase of her three-storey terrace house in Ferry Street. She looked forward to the day she would move into a modern little bungalow on the new estate at Tanniford Cross. There'd be no stairs and she'd have a fitted kitchen and a garden instead of a yard. She didn't really want to move, though. She was seventy-four and she'd lived in her house in Tanniford since the day she came to it as a young bride of eighteen.

She reached the top landing and paused to recover her breath. The front attic window gave a view of the river winding down past Alresford to the sea. She used to sit at that window when she was first married and watch for her husband coming upriver on the flood tide. By the time his Thames spritsail barge docked at Tanniford's timber port and he'd walked up from the quay, she'd have his meal ready and waiting on the table.

The landing window behind her overlooked the church-yard. She expected to be buried there in St Mary's cool green graveyard when she died, alongside her dear hus-band who'd been dead many a long year. She sighed. Her son, Lucas, was probably right. She mustn't cling to the past; and a modern little bungalow would be easier for her to manage. Besides, she had to think of Lucas too. She was lucky to have him living at home with her and he deserved something better than this old house.

She dragged a pair of stepladders leaning against the wall into position beneath the trapdoor into the loft. Clutching the lantern torch she had brought upstairs with her, she mounted the stepladder and pushed open the trapdoor. She swept the torch around the cobwebbed roofspace.

She hadn't been up there in years. The last occasion had been with a kettle of hot water to unfreeze the ballcock in the water tank one winter. She peered around the loft. There was very little up here to be sorted through and packed up. Lucas would see to it when the time came. He would organize the move. A good son was Lucas.

Suddenly, as she moved the torch about, its beam of light reflected the colour brown from a corner of the loft, causing Emily to catch her breath. *Stanford's trunk*. She'd almost forgotten it was up here. Memories of her other son swept over her, carrying her back over the years. How she'd cried then, poring over mementoes of him . . . photographs . . . school reports . . . his uniform and badges. She would ask Lucas to bring it down so she could look through all the treasures again and have a good cry before she parcelled them up for the move.

She switched off the torch, lowered the trapdoor and

descended the steps with a feeling of sadness. After all this time, the memories still hurt. It was not knowing what had happened to him that caused so much pain. Wondering if he'd lost his memory, perhaps been committed to a Home . . . a man without a name. Or maybe had an accident, his body now mouldering in a distant grave, untended . . . unknown. If she'd had a body to bury and to mourn over, she could have put Stan and her memories of him to rest. Instead, his restless spirit would wander the house, unable to settle until she found out what had prevented him returning home.

That was another reason she didn't want to move. To leave her home would be to accept that Stanford would never return. It meant abandoning her dream that one day he would come in through the front door, put his arms around her and kiss her cheek as he used to. She was reluctant to give up the dream until she knew for sure what had happened to him.

At the time, the police had tried to persuade her he'd simply left home. Perhaps emigrated to Australia. Many a young man walked out in search of a new life, they said, often without a word to his family. She'd known he wouldn't do that, though. She and Stanford had been very close, especially after her husband died.

In those last weeks before he disappeared he'd been involved in something, something he wouldn't speak about —even to her. He'd been too intent on whatever it was to just leave it and take off.

Millson picked up the next sheet of paper from his in-tray and lit another cigarette. He'd promised his daughter to try and cut down, but that phone call from his ex-wife had set him off smoking heavily again.

He started reading. It was a report about a missing person. Not the usual kind of report, though. His eyes flicked back a sentence in disbelief. *Thirty years ago?* He was being asked to look into the case of a man who disappeared thirty years ago? What did they think he was? A medium?

He continued reading. New information had come to light, it seemed. The account was garbled and Millson couldn't make head or tail of it. He went into the next room and dropped the report on Scobie's desk.

'You're good with old ladies, Norris. Use your boyish charm and find out what this old dear, Mrs Boley, is on about. Seems she's been bending the ear of the local copper about a son who went missing a long time ago. She lives in Tanniford.' He saw Scobie's face light up. 'And don't make this an excuse to spend the afternoon chatting up your girlfriend.'

Driving down the hill into Tanniford, Scobie slowed as he crossed the bridge over the railway and brought the car to a halt outside the estate agent's on the corner of Station Road and the High Street. Through the window he saw Kathy Benson's auburn head bent over her desk.

He'd met Kathy when he was working on a case in Tanniford last year and their relationship had blossomed since then. He bleeped the hooter and she looked up. He wound down the car window.

'See you later,' he mouthed at her. She nodded and smiled.

He turned into the street opposite and then down Ferry Street. The street was narrow, without pavements and the front doors of the terrace houses opened directly on to the street. Emily Boley lived at the bottom end, near the Black Dog. Scobie parked against the wall of the ironmonger's yard that was next to her house.

She opened the door before he knocked. 'You'm the police?'

He nodded. 'Detective-Sergeant Scobie.'

She sat him down in the front room where a battered brown leather trunk stood on the floor in front of the fire-place and insisted on making a pot of tea. It was a hot day and Scobie didn't really want tea, but he accepted out of politeness.

While she was in the kitchen he looked around the tiny room. There was woodworm in the floorboards and the walls showed signs of rising damp. Mrs Boley couldn't afford to maintain her house to the standard of Max Douglas's Holly Cottage.

When she returned with the tea Scobie discovered it had been brewed with fresh leaves, not teabags; and the taste, when it was poured from the pewter teapot, was refreshingly different. His first mouthful was a pleasant surprise and he settled back in the faded upholstered armchair, sipping appreciatively.

Emily Boley was not the dithering old woman Millson had envisaged. Seventy-four she might be, and white-haired. But she was as bright as a button, Scobie soon discovered, with a memory of long-ago events—if not of recent ones—that was as clear as crystal. She remembered every detail of the time her son, Stanford Boley, lived at home and the day he set off from the house never to return.

'I kept all Stanford's things in this trunk,' she said, raising the lid of the brown leather trunk. Scobie saw a neatly-pressed khaki uniform with sergeant's chevrons and a peaked cap.

Scobie put down his cup and took out his notebook. 'Your son was in the army?'

'Sergeant-instructor,' she said proudly. 'He was stationed at Colchester Barracks. Training National Service lads then, he was.'

Mrs Boley reached into the trunk and brought out a postcard-sized black-and-white photograph. She passed it to Scobie. 'This was taken the year before he went missing. He was twenty-six then.'

Scobie did a calculation. Stanford Boley—if he was alive —would be fifty-six now.

A hard-faced man in army uniform, peaked cap low over

the eyes like a guardsman's, glared fiercely at him. It was a face that must have struck terror into young recruits, Scobie thought.

'He looks very er—soldierly,' he said, handing the picture back and unable to think of a more suitable comment.

'Oh yes, every inch a soldier was Stan,' said Mrs Boley, gazing lovingly at the photograph. 'He was a regular. He joined the army as a boy cadet when he was sixteen. It became his life . . . he loved it. Broke his heart when they discharged him afore his time.'

Scobie looked up from writing. 'Why was he discharged?'

Mrs Boley shrugged. 'He told me the job was over 'cos of the end of National Service. Training was being run down and there was no post for him. He was an instructor, see?'

She fell silent for a moment, staring into space. 'Well, that's what he told me,' she went on. 'But he'd changed . . . got very secretive—and that wasn't like Stan, not with me. He went out seeing people. Said he was carrying out an investigation. Then one day he went out—same as always—and never came back.'

'When exactly was that?'

'Thirty years ago almost to the day. June 1961.'

'And you haven't heard from him since?'

'Not a word.'

'This investigation he mentioned. Do you have any idea what it was about?'

Mrs Boley's forehead creased in a frown. 'He didn't say, 'cept he was looking for a man. That's all he'd tell me. He'd been trying to find this man since the day he left the army.' Once more she stared into space. 'Something must have happened to him . . . something bad. Else he'd have come home again.'

'You reported it to the police at the time, of course?'

'Oh yes, an' they made inquiries. Then they said there weren't no evidence of a crime or he'd come to harm and they couldn't carry it no further. Told me men often took off like that without a word.' She snorted contemptuously. 'I knew it weren't like that, though.'

Scobie thought it was time to ask about her recent discovery. 'I believe you told the local constable you had some new information,' he prompted.

She nodded. 'Trouble was, I didn't know then the places Stan went to, or who he was seeing, so I couldn't tell 'em where to look. Now I do. Luke can tell you 'bout it. I'll call him.'

She shuffled to the door, put her head into the hall and shouted, 'Lukie!'

'This is Lucas, my other son,' Mrs Boley explained as a thickset man of about forty, with heavy lips and a large nose, entered the room. His dark hair was combed down over his forehead in a fringe and he was going bald at the crown. Scobie was struck by the likeness to the photograph of his brother.

Lucas Boley sat down on a chair beside his mother and seemed discomfited by Scobie's expectant gaze. He rubbed the side of his nose with his finger and looked down at his feet. Scobie wondered if the man was a bit simple.

'Tell the sergeant what you found, Lukie.'

'Yeh, OK.' Lucas Boley raised his head. 'We's moving soon, see,' he told Scobie. 'An' when I was clearing out the loft and getting Stan's trunk down for Ma, I found a package hidden up there under the water tank.'

He wasn't going to explain *why* he'd searched under the tank. As a boy, Lucas had often hidden things in the loft . . . things like sex magazines and other erotica . . . to be brought down secretly and pored over when he was alone in the house.

After he'd brought down his brother's trunk, he'd checked his old hiding-place under the water tank—more as an afterthought than in expectation of finding anything. When his fingers encountered a paper package he experienced a nostalgic frisson of excitement. He drew it out eagerly, thinking it was some forgotten sex magazines. Instead, when he unwrapped the bundle in the light of the torch, he found it contained a notebook, several official-looking letters and a map.

A glance at the notebook confirmed it was Stanford's and when Lucas read the letters he understood the reason for his brother's secrecy. He showed the notebook and map to his mother, but withheld the letters. Ma didn't need to know that, it would only upset her. Nor did the police.

'Stan must've hid the notebook and map for a reason, they must be important,' Lucas said as he explained his find to Scobie. 'And he's written down some names and addresses . . . these people must know something.' He opened the notebook at the last page that had been written on and handed it to Scobie.

Scobie glanced at the entries. There were four names and addresses. He looked up at Emily and Lucas. 'Do either of you know any of these people?' They shook their heads.

'Your son wrote them down a very long time ago,' he said doubtfully. 'I don't suppose the people live at those addresses now.'

'But you'm be able to trace 'em,' Mrs Boley said eagerly. 'And they'll tell you why Stan went to see them and what he was doing.'

Scobie looked up and met the watery eyes, shining with hope. It wouldn't take much effort to run a few checks, only an hour or two's work for a DC.

'We'll see what we can find out, Mrs Boley. I'll take the notebook and map away with me, if I may. And your son's photograph. I'll let you have them back.'

As he put them in his briefcase and rose to his feet Emily Boley laid a hand on his arm. 'I jus' want to know what happened to my son, Sergeant. You don't know what it's like not knowing a thing like that. I'm seventy-four and I want to know afore I die.'

Scobie patted her hand. 'We'll do our best, Mrs Boley.'

In the estate agent's Kathy Benson greeted Scobie with a kiss. 'What are you doing in Tanniford, Norris?'

'Mrs Boley wants us to look into the disappearance of her son—the one who went missing thirty years ago.'

'Stanford Boley. Yes, the whole village knows the story.'

'Any gossip? Rumours?'

'Not that I know of. It was back in the 'sixties and I don't suppose there are many people who would remember him now. His mother still believes he'll return one day.'

'I gather she's moving.'

'Yes. It's a pity. She's one of the original villagers. I'm handling the sale of her house and looking out for a bungalow for her.'

'I didn't go much on the other son, Lucas. He seems an odd character. What does he do?'

'He runs the local garage.'

'And lives at home?'

'Yes, always has. You mightn't think it, but he worships his mum.' Kathy glanced at her watch. 'Have you time for a coffee?'

Scobie nodded. Millson couldn't begrudge him a coffee break with Kathy.

Driving out of Tanniford later, Scobie turned off at Tanniford Cross. One of the addresses in Boley's notebook was in Elmstead Market. It would be only a small detour to make on the way back to Colchester. He decided to call there on the off chance the man Boley had named still lived there.

CHAPTER 5

On the verandah of the villa he'd rented in the hills overlooking Nerja on the Costa del Sol, a Spanish maid refilled
Max Douglas's glass from a jug of iced Sangria. In the
garden, Poppy Latimer, in a pale blue bikini, lay stretched
out on a sunbed basking in the Mediterranean sun.

She had turned up on the doorstep of his house in
Wimbledon the day after the inquest. A slim, elfin blonde
in tank top and jeans, wearing trainers and white ankle
socks, her hair in a pony tail.

'I'm Poppy . . . Poppy Latimer.' She smiled, displaying
neat white teeth. 'You and me's sort of related.'

He stared at her blankly. 'I see. Won't you come in?'

As she eased past him in the hall, blonde hair brushing
his cheek, Max felt an old familiar stirring. He controlled
his expression, remembering he was supposed to be in
mourning and devastated by his wife's death.

He showed her into the lounge. She sank into a deep
armchair, blue eyes gazing up at his puzzled face. 'Didn't
Auntie D. tell you about me?'

'No.' He shook his head.

Daphne had never mentioned the girl. But that was
hardly surprising, he thought, eyeing her slim figure and
peaches and cream complexion. Daphne wouldn't have
wanted him to know about this little poppet.

'Well, I'm the daughter of Auntie D.'s first husband,
see?'

Max started with shock, then frowned. 'My wife didn't
have a stepdaughter. And I wish you'd stop calling her
"Auntie D.".'

'No, you don't understand,' Poppy said earnestly. 'I'm

illegit. Auntie D. had no idea I existed until her father died a few months back.'

When her first husband, Peter, died in a car crash, his will and financial affairs had been dealt with by Daphne's father, who was a solicitor. He'd found a scribbled note pinned to the will. In the note, Peter bequeathed a quarter of his estate to an illegitimate daughter, Poppy Latimer . . . Latimer being the name of the girl's mother.

The discovery that his son-in-law had not only had a mistress, but had sired a child, came as a great shock to Daphne's father. He realized the knowledge would cause pain and humiliation to his daughter and when he saw Peter's signature had not been witnessed and the note had therefore no legal force, he decided to keep quiet about it.

Daphne had learned of Poppy's existence years later. Her father told her about the note six months ago as he lay dying in hospital. Although Daphne was astounded at the revelation of her former husband's child, she felt no resentment after such a long time, only a nagging guilt. Whatever the legal justification for her father's action, she felt as though she herself had stolen the bequest that rightly belonged to Peter's daughter.

Poppy would be eighteen now. Daphne decided to find her and make amends. She engaged a private detective. It took him some time to trace the girl. Eventually he found her living with her mother and a stepfather in a basement flat in Brixton. Her circumstances were miserable, he reported. The stepfather was a heavy drinker and Poppy didn't get along with him.

Daphne had the detective arrange a meeting between her and the girl. Poppy's mother had told Poppy her father had been killed in a car crash when she was little and that he'd had no family. When Daphne told her, as tactfully as she could, he'd been married to her at the time she was born, Poppy grinned.

'Mum always skates around the affair she had with my dad. I guessed it was something like that.'

'Do you mind?'

'No. Don't mean a thing to me.'

Without mentioning Peter's note, Daphne explained she'd only recently learned of Poppy's existence and had been curious to meet her. Poppy told her she was studying drama and she wanted to become an actress. At present she was working in a florist's, trying to save enough money to leave home and attend drama school.

Daphne took a liking to Poppy. Despite her home conditions, she was a bright, lively girl. And tough. A girl who would win through, given the chance.

She invited Poppy to lunch at her house when Max was at work. On this occasion she told her about the note attached to Peter's will; that it wasn't legal and her father hadn't told her about it until recently. Now, belatedly, she would like to put matters right.

Poppy, listening wide-eyed, couldn't believe her good fortune. 'You mean you're gonna give me money?'

'It's what your father meant you to have, Poppy.'

'Cor!' Poppy's eyes sparkled. 'How much?'

Daphne smiled. 'Quite a lot. I think it would be best if I set up a trust fund for you.'

Poppy's face dropped. 'I won't get anything right away, then?'

'Not until I've arranged things with my solicitors. Why? Do you need money now?'

'Not half I do! Things are terrible at home,' Poppy said fiercely. 'My stepfather's getting a right pest. I've just got to move out.'

Daphne compressed her lips. She would have liked to invite the girl to come and live with her, but it would be asking for trouble. She wouldn't have a moment's peace with Max and this pretty teenager under the same roof. She had no intention of even telling Max about Poppy Latimer.

'Come and see me next week and I'll have a cheque ready
for you. You'll be able to set up in a place of your own.'

'So you see, Auntie D. promised me enough money to leave
home and live on my own while she arranged this trust
fund for me,' Poppy told Max Douglas.

'My wife never mentioned a word of this to me.' He'd
listened attentively to Poppy's story and wondered if the
girl was trying to put over an elaborate confidence trick.

'Well, it's true,' Poppy said sharply. 'There must be
something about it somewhere. In Auntie D.'s letters, perhaps. Have you been through her things?'

'Not yet.'

He'd scanned Daphne's will to make sure it was in order
and everything came to him before he killed her. He hadn't
bothered with anything else.

'Well, would you, please? I'm desperate for that money.
I was relying on it.'

She'd already burnt her boats and told them she was
moving out. 'Keep your sodding paws to yourself!' she'd
told her stepfather when he became sickeningly affection-
ate, begging her to stay. Every day would be a battle from
now on.

'I must have it,' she said urgently.

Max needed time to think and to find out what Daphne
had been up to. From what the girl said, it sounded as
though Daphne had planned to hand over a large sum.

'I'll go through my wife's papers this afternoon,' he
promised. 'Where can I get in touch with you?'

'It'd be best if you phoned me at work. It's a florist's.'
She opened her handbag and foraged inside. 'Here . . .' She
handed him a card. 'You can phone me there.'

He glanced at it. 'Putney? That's handy. I could order
the flowers for the funeral from there.'

'Would you tell them you got their name from me?' she
said eagerly. 'Then I'll get commission.'

'Yes, of course I will, Poppy.' He gave her a warm smile.

As soon as she left he hunted through Daphne's desk in the study. He found a letter she'd begun drafting to her solicitors that bore out the girl's story. Daphne had asked a number of questions about setting up a trust fund and clipped to the draft was a signed cheque for two thousand pounds made out to Poppy Latimer. It didn't look as if she'd actually instructed the solicitors, though.

He rang them to make sure. No, they had not received any instructions of that nature from the late Mrs Douglas. Max put down the phone and sat with the draft letter and cheque in his hand, thinking.

He was now extremely wealthy. In addition to Daphne's own assets there had been the substantial shareholdings she'd recently inherited from her father. He could honour Daphne's promises to the girl without even noticing the cost. As he thought about it, he recalled the sensation of her hair brushing his face . . . her wide blue eyes . . . the emotions awakened by her visit.

Max Douglas let out a long sigh. Desire had been suppressed for such a long time . . . for twelve whole months while he was setting the scene for Daphne's death. No need for restraint now, though. He was a free man. Poppy Latimer was young, delightfully young. And she needed money . . . desperately.

With a sardonic smile he tore up the cheque and the letter and dropped them in the wastepaper basket.

The next morning Max telephoned Poppy at the florist's. She came to the phone breathless and eager.

'Have you found the cheque?'

'I'm sorry, my dear, no.'

'Something about the trust fund, then?'

'I'm afraid there's no mention of it. I suppose Daphne hadn't got around to it yet.'

'Oh.' Poppy was devastated. She could believe Auntie D.

might not have made out the cheque yet, but she couldn't believe there was nothing about the trust fund, no indication anywhere of her intentions.

'Look . . . um . . . perhaps *I* can help you.' His voice was heavy with concern. 'Can we meet somewhere? Let me take you to lunch.'

At the other end of the line Poppy Latimer's eyebrows came together sharply. She kept her tone neutral.

'OK. My lunch-break is one till two.'

'I'll pick you up at the shop. I can order the flowers at the same time.'

He took her to an expensive restaurant overlooking the Thames. She was wearing jeans and a sweat shirt and during the taxi-ride there he amused himself visualizing how he would dress her in future. She wasn't a raving beauty but she'd look stunning in fashionable clothes and with a decent hair-do, he decided.

After he'd ordered and they were sipping an apéritif, he asked her what her situation was at home.

'Bloody,' she said.

He nodded sympathetically. 'And this job at the florist's. Is it permanent?'

'No, it's just for the vacation. I'm hoping to start at college in the autumn.'

'You're a student?'

'Yes . . . a drama student.'

'How interesting,' Max murmured.

He discoursed for a while on the theatre and recent plays he'd been to. Other young girls might have been swayed by his smiling charm. Poppy Latimer was unimpressed, waiting to discover what he was leading up to.

A waiter brought the wine-list. Max made his selection and handed it back.

'About this money business,' he said. 'You see my difficulty, don't you? I mean, I'm sure you're a truthful girl, my dear, but legally . . . Well, legally you don't have the slightest claim.'

'No, I suppose not.'

She'd already checked that out with a solicitor. 'Fine words butter no parsnips,' he'd said when she explained Daphne's promises. Which turned out to mean she hadn't a hope—unless she could come up with some written evidence. And then only maybe.

Max's mild blue eyes beamed warmth and concern at her. 'However . . . in the circumstances I can't help feeling a certain responsibility for you.' He cleared his throat. 'Perhaps we could come to some . . . er . . . arrangement?'

She met his eyes. 'Arrangement? What sort of arrangement?' But she already had a good idea from the conversation so far and the expression on his face.

The waiter returned, showed Max the label on the bottle of wine, opened it and poured a sample for his approval. Max took a sip and nodded. He waited until their glasses had been filled and then went on, casually:

'I'm thinking of taking a holiday abroad after the funeral . . . to get over my wife's death. It was a terrible shock, you know, and I'd like to go away for a while.'

In fact, he intended to sell up and rearrange his life completely. The holiday would be just the start.

'Not much fun on my own, though.' His eyes sought hers. 'I was wondering . . .'

Yes, that's exactly what she'd thought. She lowered her eyes to the tablecloth. It was unfair. She'd been deprived of her inheritance. First by her father's carelessness over his will; then by Auntie D. getting drowned; and now by this man. She was certain he was lying to her about not finding anything among Auntie D.'s papers. There *must* have been a letter or a note of some kind that confirmed her story.

And now he had the nerve to proposition her just days after his wife died. Fighting back her anger, Poppy forced herself to think calmly. The way Auntie D. had been talking, the money involved ran into thousands. She wasn't going to let it slip away from her. There had to be a way of retrieving the situation. If she rejected his invitation she would never see a penny of her money, that was for sure. Her best chance was to keep in with him.

She knew from the look in Max Douglas's eyes what the invitation entailed so far as he was concerned. She considered it with cold calculation. Could she do it? He was old enough to be her father. Apart from deceiving her about the money, though, he seemed nice enough. Bearable, anyway. Could she play the part successfully? Just about, she reckoned. More important, could she manage to hold him off while she found a way to obtain what was rightfully hers. That would be the problem. She bit her lip uncertainly.

Watching her reaction, Max murmured quietly, 'No strings attached, Poppy . . . I promise you.'

She kept a straight face. Did he think she was born yesterday? He was lying, of course. But this gave her an out if she found she couldn't handle things. Anyway, she simply had to get away from her stepfather and escape from her grotty home and grotty neighbourhood. If nothing else, she'd achieve that.

Carefully composing her expression, she looked up. 'Yes, all right, I'll come away with you. That's what you want, isn't it?'

Max hadn't thought it would be so easy and he was disconcerted by her ready acceptance. He didn't stop to analyze it. She was willing and that was all that mattered. Once he had her to himself he'd soon win her over. He couldn't wait to make up for a year of boring faithfulness to Daphne.

He smiled and raised his glass. 'To us, then, Poppy.'

'To us, Maxie.' She raised her glass and winked at him.

She'd play the part for all she was worth. Just until she found a way to recover her money.

CHAPTER 6

The address in Elmstead Market was a modest semi-detached built in the 'fifties, situated in a turning off the A604 to Harwich.

A middle-aged man with thinning brown hair opened the door. He was short and stocky and wore tan corduroys.

'Mr White, by any chance?' Scobie asked.

'Yes, that's me.'

'Detective-Sergeant Scobie.' Scobie showed his warrant card. 'It's a long shot, but I'm making inquiries about a Mr Boley and I wondered if you could help me.'

The man's forehead creased in a frown. 'Boley? The only Boley I knew was a Sergeant Boley in the army—and that was donkey's years ago.'

'That would be the man,' Scobie said.

Colin White's eyebrows lifted. 'Really? Well, you'd better come in.'

He showed Scobie into a lounge. The furniture was faded and worn and looked as though it had been bought second-hand. A woman with mouse-coloured hair sat in an arm-chair watching television.

'This policeman is asking about someone I knew in the army, dear,' White told her. He turned to Scobie. 'Would you like a cup of tea or something?'

'No, thanks. I've just had coffee.'

The woman stood up and switched off the television. 'I'll leave you to it, then,' she said and left the room.

White motioned Scobie to a chair and they sat down. 'So, what about Boley?'

'It seems he disappeared . . . a long time ago,' Scobie said. 'We'd like to find out what happened to him and put his mother's mind at rest.'

White's mouth curved in mock disbelief. 'Boley had a mother?'

'Doesn't everyone?'

White snorted. 'Not men like Boley. He was a devil. Regular army type . . . and hated us conscripts. You can't believe men like him ever had a mother. But why come to me about him?'

'Your name and address was written in his notebook.'

'Oh?' Scobie saw a flash of alarm cross White's face. 'How very odd. I haven't seen or heard of the man since I did National Service.'

'That's around the time I'm inquiring about.' Scobie took out his notebook. 'Can you remember if he called on you in 1961?'

'1961? That's a long time ago.' White looked startled. 'Well, yes, he did as a matter of fact, a month or two after I was demobbed. He was in civvy clothes, I remember, and I'd never seen him out of uniform before.'

'Do you mind telling me what he came to see you about?'

Colin White gazed up at the ceiling as though trying to remember, but Scobie had the feeling it was to give him time to think.

White's eyes returned from the ceiling. 'Boley said he was investigating a crime—a very serious crime, he called it. And then he began questioning me about an exercise we'd been on. A night exercise at the end of our training course. Over at Fingringhoe. He made me go over it with him again and again—every detail—on a map he had with him.'

Scobie opened his briefcase. He pulled out the map that had been hidden in Emily Boley's loft and showed it to White. 'A map like this?'

Colin White lifted a pair of half-moon reading glasses from the table beside him and carefully fitted the wire side-pieces over his ears. 'It was a long time ago, you know.' He took the map from Scobie and scrutinized it. 'Good Lord!

Yes. That looks exactly like the one Boley showed me,' he said, handing the map back.

'Did he explain *why* he was questioning you about the exercise?'

White hesitated. 'He didn't say exactly. I had the impression someone had been injured . . . seriously. I thought perhaps someone had been shot.'

'*Shot?*'

White smiled thinly at Scobie's surprise. 'There were accidents on army exercises, Sergeant. Especially the ones at night with live ammo flying about. "Battle inoculation", it was called and they were allowed a certain percentage of casualties by the War Office. Wouldn't get away with it these days, of course. The public wouldn't stand for it and the media would howl for an inquiry.'

Scobie brought out Boley's notebook and opened it at the page containing the names and addresses. He showed the page to White. 'Do you know any of the other people, Mr White?'

White appeared to consider them carefully. Eventually he said, 'The two men . . . Mortimer and Eric Shand . . . were on the same training course I was on. The girl . . . Ruth Jones . . . was a WRAC medical orderly in the sick bay.'

'Would you have an up to date address for any of them?'

'No. We didn't keep in touch.'

'And you haven't heard of or seen any of them since?'

White hesitated. 'Well . . . yes . . . one. I came across Ruth Jones a month or two ago—quite by accident—when my wife was attending the County Hospital in Colchester. Ruth is a ward sister at the hospital. We had a brief chat. She enrolled as a nurse when she left the WRAC and has been there ever since. I think she said she lives in Marks Tey.'

Scobie made a note in his book. 'Do you have any idea why Mr Boley might have been visiting her or the other two men?'

'I suppose it was for the same reason he gave me. He was investigating something that happened on that night exercise. Look, I don't understand why you're asking questions about a visit a man made to me thirty years ago.'

'That's when he disappeared.'

'Really? Then why are you inquiring about him now, after all this time?'

'We've received fresh information.'

White suddenly looked wary. 'Does that mean . . . ?' He tailed off and began again. 'Is this a murder inquiry, then?'

'No. We don't know what happened to him yet.'

'Well, don't take any notice of what I said earlier about him. We thought every army sergeant was a monster. We were young rookies, remember, scared out of our wits of a few stripes. Makes you laugh now, doesn't it?' He wasn't smiling, though.

'Is there anything else you can tell me?'

'I'm afraid not.'

'Well, thank you for your help, Mr White. If you remember anything more give me a call. Colchester police station . . . ask for CID.'

'Yes . . . yes, I will.' He followed Scobie to the door. 'I expect you'll be calling on Ruth Jones. I hope you won't let on it was me told you where to find her.'

'Any particular reason?'

'No. I'd just rather she didn't know.'

'Very well.'

White closed the door behind Scobie and sagged against it in relief. Mortimer . . . Ruth Jones . . . himself . . . and Shand. He smiled grimly. So Boley had been after Eric Shand too, had he? Little Eric with the big brown eyes and the baby face.

He wouldn't look like that now, of course. Except for the eyes, perhaps.

*

That evening, in his flat overlooking the Castle Park in Colchester, Norris Scobie went through Stanford Boley's notebook page by page. The writing was spidery and difficult to read in places. However, it soon became apparent to Scobie that Boley had started with a long list of names and whittled it down by a process of elimination. As he turned the pages, Scobie was able to decipher scrawled comments on why this or that person had been crossed off the list.

Eventually, on the page preceding their names and addresses, Boley had set out his final list.

Opportunity	*Motive*
E. Shand	Yes
C. White	
W. Mortimer ⎬	?Ruth Jones
Corporal Tilley	Yes

Scobie frowned at the headings. Opportunity and motive for what?

At places in the notes there had been references to the sketch map. He unfolded the map and studied it. It was well-drawn and contained a lot of detail, probably traced from a large scale Ordnance survey map, Scobie thought. Natural features like hedgerows and trees had been added in crayon and at various points on the map crosses had been marked and a name written against each. Among the names were the three men on Boley's list: White, Mortimer and Shand.

Straight lines had been drawn from each position to one marked 'Sgt Boley'. There were also dotted lines leading from each position to Boley's, which followed the hedgerows and trees. Every line had a distance in yards and a 24-hour-clock time entered against it.

Scobie ran his eye over the times. They were all in the small hours of the morning, between 0200 and 0300. A time had also been written against Boley's position: 0225. Was that when whatever Boley was investigating had occurred?

'Whenever I see that soupy look on your face, Norris,' Millson said next morning as Scobie entered his office, 'I know you're about to tell me something I don't want to hear. How did you get on with Mrs Boley? Patted her hand and told her there was nothing we could do?'

'No, I didn't.'

'Didn't what? Didn't pat her hand or didn't tell her there was nothing we could do?'

'Neither. I said we'd try and find out what happened to her son. And from what she's told me, I'd say we have to.'

Millson sighed. 'All right then, sit down and let's have it.'

Scobie pulled up a chair and laid Boley's notebook and map on Millson's desk. 'The old lady's put her house up for sale and when her other son was clearing out the loft, he found this notebook and map belonging to his brother hidden up there.'

Scobie went on to report his interview with Mrs Boley and Lucas and his subsequent call on Colin White at Elmstead Market.

'I went through the notebook yesterday evening. It's clear that when he disappeared, Boley was searching for someone. White thinks it was in connection with an accident that happened during an army night exercise at Fingringhoe in 1961. Take a look at this.' Scobie opened the map and spread it in front of Millson.

Millson stretched out a hand to his packet of cigarettes lying on the desk, then withdrew it again. 'I promised Dena I'd cut down.' He gave a rueful laugh. 'I think she's afraid I'll pop off and she'll end up back with her mum.'

'Have you heard anything more from your ex-wife?'

'No. I think she was trying it on.' Millson peered down at the map. 'What's all this, then?'

'White thought Boley might have been investigating a shooting accident. Apparently, they sometimes had casualties on those battle exercises. I wondered if it was Boley who'd been injured and those straight lines could be lines of fire.'

Millson raised his eyebrows. 'At night?'

'I was supposing someone loosed off a round accidentally in the dark and Boley was trying to work out where it came from.'

Millson bent over the map and shook his head. 'No, I think the straight lines simply indicate the minimum distance between each man's position and Boley's and the shortest time it would take them to reach him. But you'll notice the dotted lines follow hedgerows and trees. I reckon those mark the actual routes the men would have to take to approach Boley's position. So perhaps someone crept up on him in the dark and took a shot at him at close range. Nasty.'

'Yes, well, take a look at this.' Scobie opened the notebook at a page and placed it in front of Millson.

Millson stared at it. '"Opportunity" . . . "Motive" . . . who wrote this?'

'Boley. That's his notebook.'

Millson puffed out his cheeks. 'This is his list of suspects, then.'

'I suppose so. Though, if he'd been shot, I would have thought his mother would have known. So that can't be the reason he was discharged from the army.'

'You mean she doesn't know why he was discharged?' Millson asked sharply.

'Well, *he* told her the job had folded up with the end of National Service. She didn't really believe it, though.'

'H'm.' Millson reached for the cigarettes again. 'Can't stop altogether,' he muttered. He put one in his mouth and

lit it, inhaling deeply. He picked up the notebook and with
the cigarette clamped between his lips he continued drawing on it, making the tip glow bright red as he turned the
pages of Boley's notes. Coming to the end, he dropped
the notebook on the desk and stubbed out the remains of
the cigarette in an ashtray. He brushed ash from his waist-
coat and looked up at Scobie.

'Boley was looking for someone all right. And he put in
a lot of hard work trying to identify him. These notes don't
give a clue as to why, though.' Millson rubbed the end of
his chin thoughtfully. 'You're right, Norris, we're obliged
to follow this up. Get on to army records and find out why
Boley was discharged. And have someone make a search of
the Death Registers at St Catherine's House. It wouldn't
be the first time a missing person has turned out to be
respectably dead without his family knowing.'

He picked up the notebook again and turned to the page
containing Boley's list. 'I wonder why this Ruth Jones is
down as a motive?'

'According to White, she was a medical orderly in
the barracks sick bay. He met her again recently. She's
now a nursing sister at the County Hospital here in
Colchester.'

'And the other two men?'

'He doesn't know where they are now. We're trying to
trace them through the DSS.'

Millson gave a snort of disgust. 'You won't get much
help from them unless it's a murder inquiry.'

'I think I may have given them the impression it is,'
Scobie said airily.

Millson gave him a look and shook his head in a pretence
of disapproval. 'Arrange an interview with Ruth Jones. Not
at the hospital. We'd probably find ourselves being slotted
in between operations or something. Make it at her home
when she's off duty.'

*

Ruth Jones's detached bungalow at Marks Tey, five miles out of Colchester, had a neat, well-kept garden. Ruth Jones too looked neat and well-kept as she opened the door. Her straight black hair was cut in a bob and she looked younger than her forty-eight years. The plain navy-blue dress had a white collar and cuffs and she wore dark blue tights.

She greeted them with a friendly smile, the trace of a Welsh lilt in her voice. The smile quickly faded when Millson explained they were making inquiries about a man called Stanford Boley and her manner became distant.

'Yes, I knew Sergeant Boley by name—as I knew most of the instructors at the barracks. And I expect I must have spoken to him at times in the course of my duties. But there's absolutely nothing I can tell you about him, though. I'm afraid you've had a wasted journey, Chief Inspector.'

'Uh-huh.' Millson was unmoved. 'I'd still like to ask you a few questions. May we come in?'

'If you wish.' Reluctantly, she led them into a sitting-room and sat them down.

'I'd like you to look at some names, Miss—er . . . Is it "Miss or "Sister" off duty?' asked Millson.

The clinically tidy room with its spotless modern furniture bore no sign of a male presence and Millson wanted to ascertain if there was a man in her life. Ruth Jones was an attractive woman and one reason for her name being under 'motive' on Boley's list might be jealousy, a passion that could lead to revenge.

'"Miss Jones" will do fine, thank you,' she said. Which told him nothing about her past and nothing about her status now.

He nodded and held out his hand to Scobie, who produced Boley's notebook from his briefcase and passed it to him. Millson opened it at the page showing the four names and handed the notebook to Ruth Jones.

'What do you make of that list of names, Miss Jones? You'll notice yours is one of them.'

She stared intently at the page, examining it in the way she might have examined a contaminated dressing at the hospital. When she looked up her face was blank.

'I make nothing of it, Chief Inspector. And I have absolutely no idea why Sergeant Boley should have written my name there.'

She handed the notebook back to him, placed her hands in her lap and crossed her ankles. They were slim ankles, Millson noticed. He admired slim ankles in a woman.

'Did I say Boley wrote those names?' he asked.

'No, but I assume the notebook is his,' she said calmly. 'It has a crown on the cover and it looks like service issue to me.'

'Very observant of you,' Millson commented. 'Why d'you think he linked you with W. Mortimer and C. White? And why should he put your name under the heading "motive" —as though you were the cause of some action by them?'

Millson had expected a reaction from her, but she met his questioning eyes without a flicker of emotion.

'I follow your line of thought, Mr Millson, but I can offer no explanation. Mortimer and White were trainees I went out with a few times. I can't even remember what they looked like now. I was young then . . . eighteen . . . and I went out with lots of soldiers. To the cinema . . . dances . . . parties.' She gave a slight smile.

Yes, and a right little raver you were, I'll bet, Millson thought, returning her smile. 'Did you know Sergeant Boley was discharged from the army about two months after the course these men were on ended?'

For the first time she seemed to hesitate. 'I heard he'd left the army, yes.'

'Did he call on you at that time? This would be in 1961.'

'He most certainly did not,' she said firmly.

'Do you know why he was discharged?'

'No, why should I?' Her tone was sharp.

'I just thought you might,' Millson said mildly. 'I don't

imagine it was an everyday occurrence for a sergeant to be
discharged in the middle of his career. Because that's what
seems to have happened.'

'I'm sure army records will be able to provide you with
information about that,' she said, in the tone of a hospital
sister admonishing a patient for asking irrelevant questions.

'She must have been a very pretty girl,' Millson said as he
negotiated the roundabout at Marks Tey and took the slip
road on to the A12. 'She's very attractive now, come to
that.'

Scobie glanced sideways at him. It was unusual for
George Millson to comment on a woman's looks. Ruth
Jones obviously appealed to him.

'She must have some idea why she was on Boley's list,'
he said. 'Yet she didn't even offer a suggestion.'

'She didn't offer anything, Norris, if you noticed. Not a
damned thing. She was very careful in what she said, very
careful indeed. There's something she doesn't want us to
find out. Did you ask White about this list?'

'No, I hadn't seen it then. I just showed him the names
and addresses on the last page.'

'Then let's show it to him and ask why Ruth Jones was
the motive for whatever it was he had the opportunity to
do.'

CHAPTER 7

After the funeral, Max Douglas had gone over his wife's
affairs with his accountant and discovered that the sum of
money Daphne had planned to settle on Poppy Latimer
was considerable. He felt no guilt in depriving Poppy of the
money, nor in deceiving her. Guilt was not in Max Douglas's repertoire of emotions. Nor did he see anything

immoral in turning her desperate need of money to his advantage.

He intended his escapade to the Costa del Sol with Poppy to be a temporary affair. At the end of the holiday he would give her a generous parting gift and dump her. It would be an exciting diversion while he replanned his life without Daphne. He felt no remorse for his wife's murder. It had been necessary to kill her and he'd done it without a qualm, even deriving satisfaction from the clever way he'd dispatched her without risk to himself.

Poppy had met him at the airport carrying a small holdall containing little more than a pair of jeans, a swimming costume and a T-shirt. He'd enjoyed buying clothes and accessories for her in the fashionable shops in Malaga. With good clothes and a visit to a Spanish hairdresser he'd transformed Poppy into an alluring young woman.

Max Douglas's joy would have been unbounded, except for a problem. The more desirable Poppy became, the more he wanted her. And the harder he tried to win her, the more unattainable she made herself. She was unmoved by the expensive gifts he lavished upon her and seemed totally immune to his charm. Max was frustrated. He'd been so sure she'd be an easy conquest.

Force was out of the question. It was not his style. He should have reneged on his promise right at the beginning and given her an ultimatum: either surrender or he'd send her home.

It was too late for that now, however, and Max found himself in a dilemna. He was becoming attached to Poppy. More than that, he admitted. He was hooked—infatuated with her.

He raised his sunglasses and looked across to where she was sunbathing in the garden as usual, her fair skin an attractive shade of brown. As he watched, she sat up from the sunbed and removed the top half of her bikini, then lay down again, exposing her breasts to the sun.

After a while Max said, 'Time for our siesta, Poppy.'

Her golden head lifted from the sunbed. She knew what that meant. Another tussle in the bedroom, needing all her wiles to keep him at bay. So far, he'd treated these romps as an amusing game, but he was showing increasing impatience and she feared he would soon force a showdown. She was surprised he hadn't already.

She turned over on to her front, soft breasts compressing against the sunbed. 'Later, Maxie, I haven't finished doing my back.' She lowered her face into the crook of her arm.

He picked up a magazine and began reading, containing his desire with difficulty. He was bent on success with Poppy, but at a loss as to how to achieve it. Clearly, it would take longer than he'd anticipated. He laid down the magazine and closed his eyes, contemplating a new idea.

He arrived at a decision and opened his eyes. She'd moved from the sunbed and was squatting on the patio painting her toenails. Adorable, he thought. Young and adorable. He couldn't remember Daphne ever painting her toenails.

'Poppy, I have a lovely little cottage in East Anglia. How about spending some time there with me after this holiday?'

She looked up from her task, considering. She'd be on safer ground there, an easier place to run from than here.

She frowned. 'I thought you said you'd flogged everything.'

'I have. Not the cottage, though. I needed a place to keep all my belongings.'

Poppy looked down at her feet again. This was her chance to search through his things for proof of Auntie D.'s intentions and face him with it. She dipped the brush in the bottle of nail varnish and carefully applied it to her little toe.

'Yes . . . sure. I'll come,' she said. 'Why not?'

Max's mouth relaxed in a smile. Patience was all he needed now.

*

Millson and Scobie's visit to Colin White had to be postponed. He was away in the Midlands on business for a week, his wife informed Scobie on the phone.

Two days later the Department of Social Security notified an address for one of the men on Boley's list: E. Shand. With the whole adult population of the UK on computer file (apart from illegal immigrants and those not having a National Insurance number for some reason) it was possible—especially given an approximate year of birth and a period of military service—to come up with a last known address. It took a lot of computer time to find it, though, and the address was often years out of date.

In Eric Shand's case it proved to be his current address. Scobie looked up his phone number and made an appointment for the next evening.

'Any theories about him?' Millson asked Scobie as he took the slip road off the A12 to Feering on the way to Shand's address at Kelvedon.

'Well, I suppose his name's under "opportunity" in Boley's notebook for the same reason the others are there. He was close to Boley's position on the exercise. And I reckon the time against Boley's name was when the accident—or whatever it was—occurred.'

'Maybe it was the cause of him being thrown out of the army.'

'And if Boley was found guilty of negligence, say . . . and dishonourably discharged . . . that would explain why he didn't tell his mother,' Scobie said.

Millson slowed as they approached the bridge over the Blackwater and nodded at a pub sign. 'We'll have a beer and a bite in there on the way back. They serve garlic bread.'

'Keep the vampires away, eh?'

'Garlic is a recognized medicinal remedy,' Millson said sternly.

He drove on through the village. 'If Boley was kicked out of the army for some offence he was alleged to have committed,' he continued, 'he could have been gathering evidence from these men to prove his innocence.'

Scobie nodded agreement. 'And when he called on White it wasn't an *official* investigation. He'd already been discharged.'

'Then what?' Millson asked. 'One of them killed him to keep him quiet? We don't even know he's dead.'

'Not officially, anyway. They haven't found him in the Register of Deaths.'

'Which means he could be alive and this could all be a waste of time.' Millson sounded resentful.

'Mrs Boley wouldn't think so, if we found him,' Scobie said.

'We're not a missing persons bureau, Norris. Our business is crime. No crime . . . no case. And, so far, we don't have any evidence of a crime.'

Eric Shand lived in a newly-built chalet not far from Kelvedon station from where he commuted daily to Liverpool Street and his work in the City.

He was small and slim, with brown wavy hair and wore a neat, blue business suit. He eyed Millson's powerful bulk with alarm as he opened the door to them.

'Detective Chief Inspector Millson and Detective-Sergeant Scobie,' Millson rumbled. 'I think you're expecting us. May we come in?'

'Yes. Yes, of course.' Shand spoke in a soft voice and he had a smooth, boyish face.

'Not interrupting your meal, are we?' Millson asked pleasantly as they stepped into the hall.

'No. It isn't ready yet.'

An older, balding man in a flowered T-shirt and designer

jeans, put his head out from the kitchen. 'It's Tony's turn to cook dinner this evening,' Shand explained. The man nodded to the two policemen and withdrew into the kitchen.

The living-room was furnished in a modern style. There was a glass table and the sofa and easy chairs were in black leather. Spotlights had been recessed into a black ceiling. A compact disc player stood on a cabinet and a television set hung from a pivoting arm on the wall.

Millson sank down into the sofa and Scobie took one of the easy chairs. Shand lowered himself into the other, giving a quick hitch to the knife-edge creases in his trousers as he sat down.

'What's this about?' he asked. 'On the phone they told me it was a missing person inquiry.'

'Yes, that's right,' Millson said. 'We believe you knew the man.'

'What's his name?'

'Boley.'

Scobie saw Shand flinch as though he'd been struck. His face registered shock . . . and something else. Fear. One word—a name—and thirty years later it brought a reaction of terror. Eric Shand's fingers on the arms of his chair were digging into the leather upholstery like claws.

As though this emotion had somehow communicated itself to the kitchen, Tony appeared at the door and said into the silence:

'Everything all right, Eric love?'

Eric Shand swallowed and recovered himself. 'Yes, it's OK, Tony. Go back to your cooking.'

Tony scorched the two policemen with a hostile glare and withdrew.

'I'm sorry,' Shand said to Millson. 'It was a shock, your throwing the name at me like that.'

'Why was that?'

Shand gave a sheepish smile. 'A ghost from the past.'

'Ghost?' Millson pounced on the word.

Shand's eyelids blinked rapidly. 'I only meant he was an awful person—someone I knew a very long time ago.'

'When would that be, Mr Shand?'

'While I was on National Service. He was a sergeant-instructor at Colchester Barracks and I was sent on a course there. That would be in 1961. I never saw him again.'

'You're sure?' Millson asked. 'You see he went missing that year and we think he might have visited you shortly before he disappeared.'

'Me?' Shand's voice squeaked in alarm. 'That's ridiculous! Why would he come to see me?'

'Because your name is on a list of people he was apparently calling on.'

'I don't understand.' Shand looked worried.

'Nor do we,' Millson said amiably. 'And we're hoping you can help us. Why do you think he had you on his list?'

Shand glanced away, avoiding Millson's eyes. 'I've no idea. Who were the others?'

'Let's see if you know them.' Millson signed to Scobie. Scobie took Boley's notebook from his brief case and read the names one by one.

'Ruth Jones?'

'No.' Millson was sure a flash of surprise crossed Shand's face, though.

'C. White?'

Shand shook his head. 'Don't know him.'

'W. Mortimer?'

Shand nodded. 'I think—in fact I know—Mortimer was on National Service with me. Perhaps White was too.'

'Corporal Tilley?'

'I think he was one of the instructors.'

Scobie closed the notebook. 'That's the lot.'

'D'you know where Mr Mortimer or Corporal Tilley live now?' Millson asked Shand.

'No. No, I don't.'

'And you haven't seen Mr Boley since you were on National Service?' Millson persisted.

'No, absolutely not.' There was a note of panic in Shand's voice.

'D'you remember an exercise—a night exercise—towards the end of your course at Colchester?'

'Ye-es.'

'Was there an accident of some kind during the exercise?'

'Accident?'

'Was anyone injured—a stray bullet, perhaps . . . something like that?'

'Not that I know of.' Shand had become more confident.

Millson returned to the subject of Boley's visits. 'We have a problem, you see, Mr Shand,' he said. 'We know Boley visited Mr White. And Miss Jones has told us he didn't call on her. What we need to establish is who he called on last, before he disappeared. You follow me?'

'Yes.' Shand's eyes had the expression of a rabbit caught in the headlights. 'Well, I've told you it wasn't me.'

There was a strained silence. Eventually Millson said, 'Show him the notebook, Norris.'

Scobie opened Boley's notebook again and passed it to Shand who took it from him gingerly as though it might bite him.

'Now, I'd like you to tell me, Mr Shand,' said Millson in a persuasive tone of voice, 'why your name is in a list headed "opportunity" and why the word "yes" appears against it under the heading "motive". D'you see where I mean?'

'Yes.' Eric Shand stared at the page as though mesmerized. Some time passed before he said, in a low voice, 'I don't know.' He looked sick.

'Oh come, Mr Shand. You must have some idea.'

'I've told you I don't know!' His voice rose hysterically. 'Who knows what something written thirty years ago means? It could mean anything.' He threw the notebook back at Scobie.

'It has only one meaning to me,' Millson said sternly. 'It means Mr Boley believed you had a motive for doing something and the opportunity to do it. I want to know what it was.'

'I don't know! How many times do I have to say this?'

Millson regarded him steadily for a moment before answering, 'No more times today, Mr Shand. We'll leave it there for the moment.' He heaved himself from the soft enfolding leather and stood up.

Shand rose with him. Scobie thought of David and Goliath as they stood facing each other. Goliath looked down and asked: 'Did you know Boley was discharged from the army not long after your course ended?'

'No. No, I didn't.'

'H'm.' Millson grunted. 'Well, thank you for your help, Mr Shand.' He made for the door.

As Scobie went to follow him, Shand touched his arm. 'Why is this being investigated now, Sergeant, after such a long time?'

Scobie paused. 'New information has come to light.'

Shand's eyes widened. 'What sort of information?' he whispered.

'I'm not at liberty to say,' Scobie said, employing the stock phrase for turning aside questions that were not to be answered.

He followed Millson out of the front door and down the concrete path. 'He's frightened,' he told Millson, stepping into the car.

'And he's holding out on us. I think he knows exactly why those names are on that list and what Boley was up to. He knows Ruth Jones too. He looked surprised when he heard her name.'

'What about blackmail?' Scobie asked, when they were seated over a meal in the pub Millson had pointed out.

'Suppose Boley was blackmailing them and one of them tried to kill him on that night exercise?'

'It's a thought, certainly.' Millson selected a hunk of garlic bread from the basket beside him and plastered it with garlic butter. Scobie averted his face as Millson put it in his mouth and began munching. 'There has to be a connection between those people,' Millson said, wafting garlic fumes over Scobie, 'other than them all being in Colchester Garrison at the same time.'

'You're upset, Eric, love. Those frigging coppers upset you, have they?'

'Leave it, Tony, I don't want to talk. Not now. Just leave me be.'

'Suit yourself, sweetie. Dinner's in half an hour. Hope you'll be better then. It's your favourite . . . *Soufflé au parfait.*'

The door closed and Eric Shand closed his eyes. *Boley.* He shuddered. 'Mad Boley' they'd called him. A memory came to him: Boley instructing them in bayonet-fighting . . . using the old style Lee Enfield with the long blade. Boley charging forward and driving the bayonet into the sandbag dummy with such force the lashings broke from the frame. Bearing the dummy onward impaled on the bayonet and pinning it to the ground. Planting his foot on it and snarling:

'Don't waste time trying to pull the bayonet out. Blow a hole in the bugger!'

He'd fired a live round into the stuffed body, yanked out the bayonet and jumped into the 'on guard' position, eyes blazing.

'Comes out easy then. Got it?'

Boley. Eric Shand put his head in his hands and began shaking. Questions after all these years.

CHAPTER 8

On the first morning of that course at Colchester Barracks Eric Shand had paraded with steel helmet and rifle in drizzling rain with a platoon of young servicemen. They clambered into trucks and were driven to the firing range at Fingringhoe. There they were formed up in two converging lines to make a letter 'V' pointing towards a grass bank topped by bracken and blackberry bushes. In the other direction, far away on the marshes, red flags fluttered in the breeze.

An army sergeant-instructor accompanied by a corporal stumped into the middle of the 'V' and addressed them.

'I'm Sergeant Boley and today you'll learn what it's like to be under fire!' he bawled. 'We call it "battle inoculation" 'cos it inoculates you 'gainst the real thing.' He showed his teeth. 'If you die from the inoculation we bury you in the churchyard up the road here.'

The men stared at him uncertainly. One or two smiled weakly. Boley's blue eyes blazed at them and the smiles died.

'You's in a battle zone now an' you obey my orders.' Slowly, at the top of his voice, he bellowed: 'STAND ABSOLUTELY STILL. DO NOT MOVE. I REPEAT: DO-NOT-MOVE!'

He nodded to the corporal who pointed a Very pistol skywards and fired. A red flare soared into the sky and exploded. The men, rain dripping from their steel helmets, watched the flare's slow descent. The only sound was the wind rustling the leaves of the trees in a nearby wood.

Suddenly the ground around them erupted in a hail of bullets as Bren gunners and riflemen opened fire from camouflaged positions in the surrounding mudbanks.

Bullets whined past them, some spattering the ground on the outside of the 'V', inches from their feet. Two men instinctively jumped backwards and crouched down. One of them was Eric Shand.

Boley drew his pistol. 'Get back in line, you weak-kneed wankers!' he screamed. He fired into the ground near the crouching men and they leapt back into position.

The firing continued for several minutes. When it stopped, Boley emerged from the centre of the 'V' and strutted along the line staring into each man's face. He stopped in front of Eric Shand and thrust his face forward until they were almost nose-to-nose.

'You disobeyed orders, son,' he said softly.

The man next to Shand said, 'It was the sudden shock, Sarge. You see we—'

Boley whirled on him. 'Who threw you a nut? I didn't hear anyone say "speak".'

'I was only explaining—'

'And don't call me Sarge. I'm a *sergeant*.' His voice rose in a snarl. 'And I'm God. You got that? GOD. You don't explain nothing 'less you's asked to and you don't speak 'less you's spoken to. Got that, soldier?'

The man cringed and nodded. Boley turned back to Shand. 'A few bullets whizzing about and you start wetting yourself.' His lip curled in a sneer. 'There's no place here for cowards. Next time you'll be RTU'd—returned to unit . . . failed course. Understand?'

Shand wilted under the glare of the maniacal eyes. 'Yes, Sergeant,' he whispered.

Boley's head swivelled, his gaze encompassing both youngsters. 'I hate cowards,' he growled. 'Cowards is poofs.'

It was an omen of events to come.

By the end of the first week the men were hardened to the rigorous daily routine . . . wading across rivers . . . crawling along ditches and making bayonet-charges across fields to attack enemy positions manned by instructors and other soldiers. Sergeant Boley was an ever-present tyrant, screaming abuse, exhorting them to greater effort. At the end of the day came a forced march back to camp and the blessed relief of a night's sleep.

Next morning the torture began all over again with reveillé, ablutions, breakfast and parade for inspection.

'On parade! Fall in outside! At the double!'

A clatter of rifles and steel helmets. Young Eric Shand scuttling into position.

'For inspection . . . *port arms!*'

Shand hadn't cleaned his rifle that morning. The ritual of inserting the regulation piece of four-by-two flannelette into the pullthrough, dropping the weighted cord down the barrel and pulling it through two or three times, took several minutes. Eric Shand had spent those precious minutes in his bunk, believing his rifle would pass inspection as it hadn't been fired since he cleaned it last.

Weariness had blunted his memory. Yesterday, responding to the shout of: 'Enemy aircraft! Take cover! *Down!*' he'd jumped into the nearest ditch and the muzzle of his rifle had dug into the mire at the bottom.

A corporal-instructor moved along the ranks, inspecting weapons. Shand swung the rifle forward and inserted his thumb into the open breech to reflect the light.

The corporal grasped the end of the barrel and applied his eye to it. 'I can't see a thing,' he snapped. 'Take out the bolt.'

That was the moment Eric Shand remembered his rifle barrel embedding itself in the mud of the ditch. He removed the bolt with a feeling of dread. Having an unserviceable weapon was a serious offence.

The corporal squinted down the barrel again. 'Sergeant Boley! Take a look at this.'

Boley strutted forward and took the rifle from him. Holding it skywards he applied his eye to the muzzle. 'It's full of shit!' He threw the rifle back at Shand. 'Fall out!'

Quaking, Shand stepped one pace back and marched to the rear of the parade.

The inspection over, Boley turned to one of his NCOs. 'Take over, Corporal. March the men off.'

As Boley approached him, Shand came smartly to attention. The sergeant stood in front of him, feet astride and hands clasped behind his back.

'You's in big trouble, son.' He rocked back and forth on his heels, his eyes boring into Shand's. Nervously, Shand lowered his gaze.

'Look at me!' Boley bellowed. Shand's eyes swivelled upwards again. 'You see my mouth moving?'

'Yes, Sergeant.'

'That's 'cos I'm talking to you.' Boley put a stubby finger to his eye. 'You look me right here in the eye when I'm speaking to you. Understand?'

'Yes, Sergeant.' Soft brown eyes gazed up at hard blue ones like an obedient dog.

Boley's thick lips curved slightly. 'That rifle of yours has a blocked muzzle. Know what would happen if anyone fired it? The breech 'ud burst and they'd get their face blown off.' Boley rocked on his heels. 'The CO here is a hard man . . . real hard.' He shook his head sadly. 'If I put you on a charge for this, he'll sentence you to the glasshouse.'

Boley paused, his gaze roving over Eric Shand's face. 'You'd have a bad time in the glasshouse, son. They'd love a pretty-looking lad like you . . . love you to death, they would.'

Shand stared up at him, his eyes widening.

Boley nodded. 'Oh yes, make no mistake 'bout that. On the other hand,' he went on, his voice softening, 'you can accept my punishment instead. You'll find that a deal easier, son.'

Shand swallowed, his eyes darting around like a frightened animal. There was no one in sight.

'Well? Do I put you on a fizzer and march you into the CO? Or are you gonna take my punishment?'

Shand swallowed again. 'I'll take your punishment, Sergeant.'

Boley's lips parted and he nodded towards the latrines block on the edge of the parade ground. 'In there, then.'

He followed Shand into the hut and locked the door behind them. 'Get your pack off, son.' His voice had become a croon.

'Boley was given a medical discharge,' Scobie informed Millson the day after they interviewed Eric Shand.

'On what grounds?'

'The Army Records Office won't say. I tried to find out over the phone. Some clerk prattled on about confidentiality, so I spoke to his boss. The most he would do was to forward the papers to the Senior Medical Officer at Colchester Garrison. He said we must contact him if we want to know more.'

'Damn bureaucracy,' Millson growled. 'Fix up for me to see the SMO, then.'

Boley found excuses to punish young Eric Shand several more times during the three-week course. Eric was afraid to complain to anyone or to report him. It would have been his word against a sergeant's. And Boley had warned him, with a grim smile, that if he didn't keep his mouth shut there'd be a bullet with his name on it the next time they were on the firing range.

Then, at the end of the course, the final exercise. One that lasted the whole night through.

George Millson was in a bad temper when he and Scobie arrived at the office of Major Wyndham-Thomas, the

Senior Medical Officer at Garrison Headquarters. There
had been another phone call from his ex-wife, an ultimatum
this time.

'I have legal custody of Dena,' Jean reminded him.
'Either you return her or I'll take you to court.'

'I've told you she wants to stay with me.'

'The court ordered that she live with me. How d'you
think it'll look in the papers? "Policeman abducts young
girl",' she said nastily.

'Don't be ridiculous! She's my daughter and she's here
of her own free will.' Angrily, he'd hung up.

Major Wyndham-Thomas was regarding him doubtfully.
'I'm not prepared to disclose this man's medical record to
you, Chief Inspector. I see no reason to do so. You wouldn't
like your doctor to reveal *your* medical history, would you?
H'm?' The raised eyebrows suggested it would contain
embarrassing information about Millson's physical condition.

'It wouldn't bother me if I were dead,' Millson retorted.

The Medical Officer peered at him over the tops of his
horn-rimmed spectacles. 'This man is deceased?'

'We have reason to believe so,' Millson said, avoiding
Scobie's eye.

'H'm. Well, that could make a difference, I suppose. Why
do you want to know his medical history?'

'I don't. I simply want to know the reason for his discharge.'

'He was unfit for military service.'

'I know that!' Millson struggled with a rising temper.
'Doctor, I am investigating this man's disappearance . . .
perhaps his death and I—'

'You mean he was murdered?'

Millson exploded. 'No, I don't mean he was murdered!
I don't even know for sure that he's dead. I've been told
he was given a medical discharge from the army and I need
to know why. It may have a bearing on my inquiry. Now,

will you please tell me, Major, or do I have to take this higher?'

'I see,' Major Wyndham-Thomas said in a lofty tone of voice. He stared at the wall above Millson's head for a while. Then, lowering his gaze he said grudgingly, 'Well, it's against my better judgement, but I'm going to read you the medical report on Sergeant Boley at the time he was recommended for discharge.'

He opened the folder on his desk and extracted a type-written sheet.

Boley squatted at a gap in the hedge, his rifle and forage cap on the ground beside him. He peered into the blackness, straining his ears. At the first sound of movement he would take up the rifle and fire tracer rounds into the darkness ahead of him, just above head-height. When the magazine was empty he'd move quickly away to the farm buildings over the ridge behind him and join the other instructors acting as 'enemy'. Those were the instructions given to him at the exercise briefing.

A dark figure, its face blackened and wearing a balaclava, crawled noiselessly along the side of a hedge towards him. A folded empty kitbag was stuffed inside the man's battledress blouse. He paused for an instant and looked up at the black sky. No moon tonight. Teeth flashed white in the blackened face. Boley wouldn't see a thing, not a bloody thing. The man consulted the luminous face of the field compass strapped to his wrist and slithered forward again, low to the ground.

Boley heard a rustle in the darkness behind him and stretched out a hand for his rifle. The air whispered above him and as he whirled round, the open end of a kitbag was thrust over his head and down to his waist. The drawstring was pulled tight, pinning his arms to his sides and he was pushed over on to his back.

He grunted as the air was forced from his lungs by the

weight of someone sitting astride his chest. His webbing belt was unclipped and he felt an invading hand inside his trousers. Outraged, he lashed out with booted feet. The searching hand closed viciously and Boley reared in agony. Inside the canvas kitbag his muffled scream died as he blacked out with pain.

At the exercise debriefing the following morning the Chief Instructor made only a brief reference to the incident.

'I said I wanted realism in this exercise . . . that if you caught up with the "enemy" you knew what to do.'

He'd been confident his instructors would have withdrawn before the attackers reached their positions. It seemed Sergeant Boley had been caught napping.

'Well . . . someone took my words to heart.' He gave a wry smile. 'I mustn't complain about that, but as a result I'm an instructor short.'

The Chief Instructor was by no means sure the attack on Sergeant Boley had been made by an over-enthusiastic soldier. He knew Boley was disliked by many of the instructors and there were persistent rumours about his violent behaviour. Perhaps the night exercise had provided the opportunity for someone to take revenge.

Major Wyndham-Thomas finished reading the medical report with its clinical terms and replaced it in the folder.

'In plain language, Chief Inspector, the man was neutered. The way a farmer neuters livestock . . . by crushing. It's as effective as a surgeon's scalpel.'

Neutered. Millson, not usually squeamish, repressed a shudder. After a hysterectomy, a woman could still function as a woman, even though she couldn't have children. But a man deprived of his manhood—no libido, no virility— wasn't a man at all.

'You can understand my reluctance now,' said

Wyndham-Thomas. 'It's not like being unfit through bad
eyesight or losing a limb.'

'No . . . definitely not,' said Millson. 'What effect would
it have had on Sergeant Boley—apart from the obvious
one.'

'He'd be angry, Chief Inspector,' said Major Wyndham-
Thomas, 'very angry indeed.'

Scobie said, 'But I thought neutering . . . well, with dogs
and cats . . .'

'Would make him docile?'

'Well, yes,' said Scobie.

'A common misbelief, Sergeant. Only if it's done before
puberty. After that . . .' The Major shook his head. 'Rage.
Very hard for a man to come to terms with, you see.'

'So he'd want revenge,' Millson said. 'Revenge on who-
ever did it to him.'

'I would think that very likely,' the MO agreed.

'Is there any indication among those papers that he knew
who did it?'

'No. I looked through them before you came. There was
an investigation by the Military Police at the time. Their
report concludes: "attack by person or persons unknown".'

'Well, we know now who Boley was after and why,' Millson
said, turning out of the Barracks gates into Military Road.
'My God! What a motive for revenge.'

'He'd want to kill the man,' Scobie said.

'No, Norris, not kill,' Millson said grimly. 'He'd want
revenge in kind. That's what he'd want.'

'The man who did it must have had a mighty strong
reason for doing a thing like that.'

'Yes. Which means we have two men with a savage
hatred of each other.' Millson steered the Sierra round the
St Botolph's roundabout into the one-way system. 'Question is, did Boley find his man and take revenge, then disappear to escape the consequences? Or was he killed in the

attempt? Either way, we have a murder case on our hands, Norris. A thirty-year-old murder case. I want a check on all suspicious deaths and unsolved murders in 1961 of males aged between eighteen and thirty.'

CHAPTER 9

Mavis Mortimer picked up the letter from the front door mat and saw the Spanish stamp. Holding the envelope at arm's length as though it was contagious, she bore it down the hall and into the dining-room where she and Wilfred were about to start breakfast.

'From your *friend*,' she said accusingly, dropping it beside Wilfred's plate. He was suffering what lawyers termed, 'guilt by association' or, in Mavis language, he and Max were 'two of a kind'.

Wilfred opened the letter. Max wrote as if nothing had happened. No word of apology. Simply said he was having a wonderful time and had never felt better in his life. Enclosed with the letter was a photo of Max on the beach with his arm round Poppy. She wore a minuscule bikini and round her neck hung a gold chain. As Wilfred gazed at the photo Mavis suddenly snatched it from him and peered at it closely.

'*Ohh* . . .' She let out a long deep groan, a woman in pain. 'That gold chain was Daphne's. Oh, how could he? How could he give it to that young trollop?' She threw the photo at Wilfred and attacked her plate of cereal.

Wilfred gazed sourly at the virile Max in white shorts, looking bronzed and fit. Some men had all the luck. He put the photo down and read the rest of the letter. Max and Poppy were returning from Spain to the cottage at Duke's Green. By the time this letter arrived, they would probably already be there. Perhaps Wilfred would like to ring him sometime?

'He's taken Poppy to the cottage,' Wilfred told Mavis.

'*What?*' She choked on her cornflakes. 'It's enough to make poor Daphne turn in her grave.'

Not if she'd been cremated, though, Wilfred thought. Perhaps that was why Mavis was against being cremated —she wouldn't be able to revolve when he did something she disapproved of. Wilfred always assumed his wife would die before him.

Mavis emptied her mouth. 'Max was always chasing young bits of girls. He tried it on with Pamela, you know.'

No, he didn't know. Wilfred tried to recall his daughter at eighteen, but could only visualize the sober-faced thirty-year-old she was now.

'What did she do?'

'She saw him off, of course!' Mavis crunched her corn-flakes fiercely and Wilfred was reminded of the fiery young Mavis of his youth.

'Max is a pet. I adore him.' That's what Pamela used to say, Wilfred remembered. The words held a different meaning to him now. Maybe there had been more between Max Douglas and his daughter than he'd known. Wilfred thrust the uncomfortable thought aside.

'Mind you, Daphne kept Max on a tight rein these last twelve months, though,' Mavis said. She paused, a fresh spoonful of cornflakes half way to her mouth. 'You don't think there was anything funny about her death, do you?'

Wilfred was shocked. 'No! Of course not.'

The spoon continued its journey and Mavis slurped milk and flakes into her mouth. She chewed for a while. 'Very convenient for him, though, wasn't it? Left him free to run off with that girl.'

Poppy Latimer, in a dirndl skirt and sandals, walked deter-minedly to the top of the hill, clambered over a style into a field and sat down on the grass. In the valley below was Max Douglas's cottage and in the distance the village of Duke's Green. She'd walked up here to be alone and to sit and think, undisturbed.

She'd been dismayed to find that all Max and Auntie D.'s belongings from the London house were still in store and wouldn't be delivered to Holly Cottage for another two weeks. Meantime Max was becoming ever more amorous and turning on the pressure. Any day now she'd be given an 'either or' option. And since she'd take the 'or' option, it meant she'd be shown the door.

Poppy's smooth forehead creased in lines of thought as she searched furiously for a way to keep Max at bay for another two weeks without bringing about a confrontation. She had an idea. It was absurd, but she believed it would work. Could she bring it off? Well, she'd have a darned good try and she'd either succeed or fall flat on her face.

Poppy stood up and smoothed her skirt. Mouth firmly set, she walked down the hill.

In the front garden of Holly Cottage Max Douglas, in open-necked shirt and shorts, was pruning the Leylandii with an electric hedge-trimmer. He saw Poppy returning down the hillside and wondered if she liked it here. Holly Cottage was isolated—the nearest dwelling was half a mile away. The cottage was completely modernized, though, with a dream kitchen in which Daphne had had the latest and best equipment installed. Max smiled indulgently. Not that young Poppy would be interested in cooking or house-work. For that, he'd engaged a woman from the village who cycled up here every day.

As Poppy reached the gate and sauntered into the garden, Max eyed her appreciatively. Her blonde hair glinted in the sun and her cheeks were a warm pink from the walk.

Poppy saw desire flicker in his eyes. She parted her lips

in a loving smile and the desire flared into flame. Yes, it might not be too difficult, she told herself. Not for a girl who aspired to be an actress.

She made her approach the next morning when he came into her room and sat on the bed as she was dressing, a habit he'd developed in Spain.

'I don't go much on this relationship of ours, Max.'

'Hm? What do you mean?'

'There's no future in it for me.'

He said quickly, 'You're not leaving me?'

She heard the anxiety in his voice. So far, so good.

'Case of having to, isn't it? We can't go on like this.' That's really got him worried, Poppy decided, seeing the expression on Max Douglas's face.

'Why? What's the matter? I don't understand.'

Here goes, she thought. 'Well, it's obvious you want to go to bed with me,' she said and saw his mouth drop open. 'But you don't think enough of me to marry me.'

'*Marry?*' His voice rose an octave, the tone incredulous.

That's it, I've blown it, she thought. He'll never go for it. But she pressed on. 'Yes. People do, you know, Maxie. Get married, I mean.' She took off her pyjama top and turned to the wardrobe, selecting a dress.

Max watched her, masking his surprise. He hadn't considered marriage. For one thing he'd assumed she wouldn't agree to it because of their age difference. For another, he hadn't been looking for a long-term attachment.

Marriage. Max thought about it. Poppy as a permanent bedmate. Another prospect opened up. Children. Daphne hadn't wanted children and he'd agreed. He would have liked them, though.

Poppy pulled a white tiered dress from its hanger and slipped it over her head. It was one Max had chosen for her himself in Malaga. In the mirror she watched his eyes following her movements as she wriggled the dress down over her body. Demurely, she eased the pyjama bottoms off under her dress and stepped out of them. Why didn't he say something instead of sitting there looking stunned?

She said over her shoulder: 'But since you don't want to—'

'Oh, but I do! I *do*! I think it's an excellent idea,' he said enthusiastically.

Bingo! She turned round and smiled at him. 'Is that a proposal?'

'Of course it is!'

'Thank you. I accept.'

'Poppy . . . darling . . .'

Eagerly, he stepped forward and reached for her. She kept smiling as he pulled her against him and his mouth descended on hers. His hands began fondling her. Poppy steeled herself. This was the tricky part. Gently, she pushed him away.

'Not until we're married,' she said softly. 'You see I'm . . .' She gave him a shy look and lowered her eyes. 'Well . . . you know.' She managed a blush. 'So I'd like us to wait,' she murmured.

'Yes, of course, darling.' Max gazed at her adoringly, hardly able to credit his luck. This delightful and innocent young creature was soon to be his . . . and for always.

Poppy raised her eyes and read the joyful expression on his face. There, she'd done it. He was safely caged for a while.

For a long time after his marriage to Daphne, Max Douglas had been scrupulously faithful. Later on though, he began to have affairs, his frequent absences on property deals providing the opportunities. The liaisons were casual and brief—Max wasn't interested in a permanent relationship and had no intention of jeopardizing his marriage. He was content with his life. He had plenty of money, plenty of

diversions and a rich, loving wife whom he was wise enough
not to neglect.

As time passed, however, he grew careless and eventually
Daphne became suspicious. She engaged a private detective. His report, after several weeks of observation, shocked
her.

'Your husband's been dipping his wick all over the place,
Mrs Douglas. Every chance he gets, far as I can see.'

'Just the facts, if you please, without your comments,'
she said coldly.

The facts were inescapable. Max had been unfaithful
with a number of young women. The inquiry agent's written report a week later gave dates, times, names and
locations.

Daphne thought long and hard and decided she didn't
want a divorce, not at her age. She had a well-ordered social
life and she didn't relish the role of a middle-aged divorcée.
Besides, until recently Max had been a very satisfactory
bedmate and she wanted to keep him.

What to do about it, then? Confront him with the evidence? He might simply laugh . . . tell her to go to hell . . .
and carry on just the same. She couldn't bear that.

Suppose she threatened to cut off his funds? The trouble
was she didn't know how far he was dependent on her
money these days. She'd look a fool if she threatened to do
that and he told her to go ahead, it didn't matter. She'd
better make sure first.

CHAPTER 10

Two days after their meeting with the Senior Medical Officer, Millson and Scobie called on Colin White who'd then
returned from his business trip.

'Another visit?' White's eyebrows lifted when Millson

introduced himself. 'And a Chief Inspector?' He laughed nervously. 'Must be serious then about old Boley?'

'It is,' Millson said. 'And I'd like to ask you some questions.'

They sat down in the shabbily-furnished front room. 'Would you like a drink?' White's hand hovered in the air above the door of the sideboard.

Millson shook his head. 'You told Sergeant Scobie you knew Ruth Jones—had met her again recently, in fact.'

'Ye-es,'

'Was she your girlfriend when you were in the army together?'

'Good heavens no! I took her out a couple of times, that was all.'

'You see, we've now examined Sergeant Boley's note-book. In it he links her name with yours and puts hers under the heading, "motive". Why did he do that do you think?'

White's face was expressionless. 'I've no idea,' he said. 'Though I remember *he* thought she was my girlfriend too.'

'Why should that be a motive for anything?'

White shrugged. 'Jealousy? Rivals for the same girl? I don't know.'

'If you weren't her boyfriend, do you know who was?'

'Sorry, no idea.'

'What about a man called Mortimer?'

White frowned. 'Possibly. I believe he went around with Ruth a bit.'

Scobie put in a question. 'You told me Boley was investigating an accident that occurred during the exercise. Someone being injured, you thought. Did he tell you any more than that?'

'No ... though I did wonder if it was Boley himself who'd been hurt. The CO told us an instructor had been injured, so maybe it was him.'

Millson said heavily, 'It was.'

'Well, I'm not surprised,' said White. 'It would serve him right. He thought he was God.' He gave a cynical laugh. 'Told us so on the first day of the course. He was quite mad.'

'Why d'you say that?' Millson asked.

'Because he was.' White hesitated. 'He was a pervert too.'

Millson's eyebrows arched. 'Meaning?'

White's voice rose harshly. 'He was a sadist . . . a wild beast. He prowled around doing what he liked to young soldiers.'

Millson regarded him steadily. White was quivering with anger. 'Anyone in particular?'

White lowered his eyes and didn't answer for a moment. Then he said quietly, 'There were several. Eric Shand was one. Young Eric was Boley's favourite. I told him to report the swine, but he was afraid to.' He looked up at Millson. 'Was Boley badly hurt?'

'Oh yes,' Millson said bleakly, 'somebody neutered him.'

'Good God!' White caught his breath. 'Look . . . what I said about Eric Shand. Eric was a gentle lad . . . he wouldn't have done a thing like that.'

'Somebody did.'

'Chief Inspector, Boley was a maniac . . . depraved . . . he had it coming to him,' White said earnestly.

'Yes, I got the picture the first time you said it, Mr White. No one is allowed to take the law into their own hands, though.'

'No, of course not,' White muttered.

He pulled out a packet of cigarettes and put one in his mouth. He offered the packet to Millson and Scobie. Scobie, a non-smoker, shook his head and was surprised when Millson said,

'Thanks, left mine in the car,' and took one. Millson's latest idea—of curtailing his smoking by not carrying cigarettes about with him—didn't seem to be working.

The two men lit up. Millson inhaled and blew smoke out through his nostrils. 'Why didn't you tell this to Sergeant Scobie when he called?'

'I thought you might suspect me of having something to do with Boley's disappearance.'

'What makes you think we don't?'

White looked startled. 'Boley was alive and well when he left me.'

Millson frowned at him. 'We have only your word for that. According to Mr Shand and Miss Jones he never got to them, so you could be the last person he saw.'

As White's eyes rounded in alarm, Millson added mildly, 'I'm only pointing out we have no confirmation of what you say, Mr White.'

'D'you think White could have killed Boley?' Scobie asked in the car.

'I don't know about killing him. He could certainly have done the other thing,' Millson said. 'Did you see how angry he was? Even now, after all this time? It wouldn't surprise me if he'd been one of Boley's victims. One thing's for sure. If what White says is true, Shand had a mighty powerful motive for taking revenge on Boley.'

'And it explains Boley writing "yes" against his name under "motive".'

Millson nodded. 'And if Boley decided Shand was the culprit, there'd be a hell of a to-do when he caught up with him.'

'I can't see a wimp like Shand killing him, though, even in self-defence.'

Millson's mouth twitched in a brief smile. 'Tread on a worm and it will turn, Norris. Proverb.'

'I thought the saying was: "even a worm will turn".'

'Same thing. Let's go see him.'

*

On the night of the attack on him, Boley had been admitted
to the garrison sick bay and transferred the next morning
to the Essex County Hospital. From there he'd been sent
on sick leave. A fortnight later he was recalled to Colchester
Barracks for a medical examination.

'You've made a good recovery,' the Medical Officer told
him. 'However . . .' He veiled his prognosis with phrases
like 'normal in every other way' and 'other things in life
besides that'.

Boley cut him short. 'I'll be like this always, then?' He'd
cherished the hope of recovering his manhood in time.

'The condition is irreversible, I'm afraid. I'm recom-
mending a medical discharge.'

Boley didn't want a medical discharge. He didn't want
any kind of discharge. The army was his life. He was a
regular, not like those weak-kneed civvies who were in for
a couple of years' National Service. He said so, but the MO
was adamant.

'I have to consider the best interests of the Service . . .
as well as your own welfare, of course.'

By which the MO meant the psychological as well as
the physical consequences of Boley's injury. He was also
influenced by the opinion of Sergeant Boley's CO that the
army would be better off without him.

A month later, after his appeal against the decision to an
Army Medical Board had been turned down, Boley was
discharged.

A week later he was back in Colchester at the Red Lion,
telephoning an old crony at Military Police Headquarters.

The inquiry by the military police into the attack had
been thorough. The MPs regarded Boley as one of their
own kind. An uncompromising, fearless disciplinarian. And
unpopular for it, like themselves. They set out to discover
his attacker with enthusiasm and determination, taking
statements and studying the logbooks and reports of the
night exercise.

To locate Boley in the pitch blackness of that particular night had required precise knowledge of his position and the NCOs and men to whom this information was available were closely questioned. To no avail. All were able to account for themselves satisfactorily. With no other leads to follow, a formal report was made to the Garrison Commander that Sergeant Boley had been attacked by 'person or persons unknown'.

The man Boley telephoned was Sergeant Emmerson of the Military Police, a one-time drinking companion. It was Emmerson's men who had carried out the inquiry. Boley told him he was in Colchester and invited him for a drink.

They met in the bar of the Red Lion, Emmerson in uniform, Boley in his new civilian clothes.

'I gotta find out who done this to me,' Boley growled at Emmerson. 'I gotta know. Shan't rest till I do.'

Emmerson regarded him curiously. He'd read the medical reports and interviewed Boley in hospital himself after the attack. Apart from looking strange out of uniform, Boley seemed his old self.

'You're going to investigate yourself?'

'Yeh, I got all the time in the world now. I'll find out who the sod was.'

Emmerson nodded sympathetically. 'If there's anything I can do to help . . .'

'Yeh, I'd like a cag at your blokes' reports and a read of the statements. Give me somewhere to start, like.'

'I'll see what I can do,' Emmerson promised.

He met Boley in the Red Lion again the following day. As they sat down with their drinks, he produced a bundle of papers from beneath his greatcoat and passed them across the table to Boley.

'There's a copy of everything in the file—rough notes as well.'

'Thanks. Any leads?'

Emmerson stroked the toothbrush moustache he'd grown

in expectation of an interview for a commission. 'No one we could put our finger on. Obviously it was someone with a grudge against you, but you'd know better than us who that might be.'

Boley's face darkened. 'Yeh, I can think of several.'

'He knew exactly where to find you in the dark, so we reckoned it had to be someone with a close knowledge of the exercise plan, like one of the other instructors.'

One or two people he'd taken statements from had been quick to suggest a motive for what had been done to Boley, and Emmerson went on, 'He could have been annoyed about his girlfriend.'

He met Boley's eyes. They understood each other.

'Maybe,' Boley growled.

After his meeting with Emmerson, Boley called in at the barracks and sought out the corporal in charge of the orderly room. Rees was startled to see him. He knew from the confidential reports—as did others in the administration office—what had happened to Boley. Rumours had passed from mouth-to-mouth like a Russian whispering game: Boley had turned into a fag . . . he was a nancy-boy with a voice like a girl . . . he was living with another man . . . But the bleak-faced man confronting Corporal Rees was the same terrifying Boley he'd always been and Rees quailed before the maniacal eyes.

'Just come from the Military Police,' Boley told him. 'Sergeant Emmerson says you's to give me the names and home addresses of the trainees on my last course.' It wasn't true, but he knew the corporal wouldn't dare question it. 'An' I want the instructors' notes and logbooks of the night exercise.'

The course had been the final stage of two years' training and the National Servicemen on that course had now been demobbed. Boley intended to pursue them into civilian life.

*

With the information he'd gathered Boley returned to the home he shared with his mother and young brother in Tanniford and began work. Using the message logs of the exercise and the notes made by the police, he listed everyone—officers, instructors, trainees—who was within reach of his position at the time the assault on him took place. Methodically, he worked through the list, checking and re-checking, crossing off those whose statements were fully corroborated.

He arrived at a list similar to the one the military police had produced, except that he'd been able to eliminate some names because of his knowledge of the battle area. He'd deleted two of the instructors too. The police hadn't known they were bosom friends of his.

He then made another list. As soon as he regained consciousness that night Boley had started a mental catalogue of suspects, casting his mind over past incidents for who had a reason to take that sort of revenge. Now he wrote out the names.

He compared the two lists. Some names appeared on both. One was Eric Shand's. Boley considered Shand . . . remembered his moaning and weeping. Would he have had the courage to creepy-crawl up on him in the dark and attack him? Shand hated him enough. Boley nodded. Yes, Shand could have done it.

He continued his deliberations, considering the other suspects one by one and balancing the arguments for and against each. Finally he settled on four names. One of these men had been his attacker, the man who had destroyed his life. And when he found him . . . Boley's eyes glowed with rage.

Eric Shand looked more like a terrified rabbit than ever, Scobie thought, when he and Millson interviewed him in his sitting-room two days later. Shand sat on the edge of his black leather armchair, rigid and white-faced. There was no sign of his friend, Tony.

Millson had been grumpy and mostly silent on the drive from Colchester. Scobie gathered the mood was caused by a letter from his solicitor about his ex-wife's court case. Apparently, it wouldn't be so much a question of whether Millson's daughter preferred to live with him, as what the court thought was best for her. Millson would have to satisfy the court that Dena would be better cared for by him than by his ex-wife, the solicitor had warned him, and he didn't rate his chances of winning very high.

Millson eyed Shand morosely. 'Since we last spoke to you, more information has come to light,' he said. 'We now understand you had good reason to hate this man, Boley.'

'I don't know what you mean.' Eric Shand's nostrils twitched nervously.

'I think you do. Boley was a pervert and you were one of his victims. Isn't that right?'

Shand's eyes grew larger. 'Who told you?'

'We'll get along better if I ask the questions and you answer them,' Millson said tersely. 'Now . . . is it true?'

'Yes,' Shand said in a whisper, putting his hands over his ears like a child. He sat with lowered head, remembering the hard obscene hands . . . the drip of a tap in the quiet latrines. Boley's laboured breathing. Shame . . . disgust.

He raised his head and faced Millson with haunted eyes. 'Boley ruined my life.' His lower lip trembled. 'I was twenty and in three weeks he wrecked my whole life. Wrecked *me!* Do you understand?'

'Yes, I think I do.' Millson spoke gently. 'And I understand how you'd feel.'

'Do you? Do you really?' Shand asked with biting sarcasm. 'Well, I doubt it, I doubt it very much. The man was an animal . . . ravaging . . . violating . . .' He broke off.

'So you took revenge on him and then he came after you and—'

'No! I don't know what you're talking about.'

'You don't know what happened to Sergeant Boley on the night exercise?'

'No.'

Millson turned to Scobie. 'Read the medical report to him, Sergeant.'

Scobie took the copy of the typed report from his briefcase and read out the clinical description of Boley's injuries. Shand looked frightened.

'*You* did that to him, didn't you?' Millson continued relentlessly. 'Paid him out for — '

'*No!*'

'You had motive, you had opportunity — '

'It wasn't me! Anyway, I thought you said you were investigating Boley's disappearance . . . not this.'

'The two events are connected. After Boley was discharged from the army he began a hunt for the man who'd done that to him. I believe he found him . . . there was a violent confrontation . . . resulting in Boley's death.'

Eric Shand's eyes were enormous. '*You think I murdered him?*'

'Not necessarily murdered. If there was a fight, it could have been self-defence . . . perhaps an accident even. Witnesses have said he was a violent man and — '

'Stop it!' Shand shouted hysterically. 'I didn't attack Boley and he didn't come after me. I never saw him again!'

Millson heaved a loud sigh. Scobie knew it was a pretence of exasperation, intended to unnerve Shand still further. 'No one had a better motive than you, Mr Shand.'

Eric Shand's eyes darted about the room as though seeking refuge.

'Did they?' Millson demanded.

Shand's eyes momentarily met Millson's and swerved away again. 'Yes!' He sounded desperate.

'Who?'

'Wilfred Mortimer. He was on Boley's list. You told me so yourself.'

'You'll have to do better than that,' Millson said. 'Why Mortimer?'

'Boley raped his girlfriend.'

Millson eyebrows lifted sceptically. 'How d'you know?'

'Boley told me himself. He boasted about it the morning after. He was like that.'

'Who was the girl?' But Millson knew, even before Shand uttered the name.

CHAPTER 11

Detective Chief Inspector Millson was a good deal more formal when he and Scobie called on Ruth Jones the day after their interview with Eric Shand.

'The last time we were here you told us Boley was just a name to you,' he said severely. 'Someone you may have spoken to a few times, but nothing more. Is that correct?'

'Yes.' Her tone was curt. Today she was wearing a sleeveless, full-skirted dress with a floral pattern and her dark hair looked freshly-washed and set.

Millson continued his formal tone of voice. 'Recent information I have received leads me to believe you have cause to remember the man only too well.'

Scobie noticed her eyes flicker slightly. Her voice was steady, though, when she spoke.

'What exactly does that mean, Chief Inspector?'

Millson said bluntly, 'I've been told he raped you.'

Her eyes widened, but there was no way of knowing whether it was with shock at the statement, or alarm at their knowledge. Whichever it was, she recovered quickly.

'That's ridiculous! Who told you that?'

'Never mind who told me, Miss Jones, is it true?'

'Of course not!' Her chin rose defiantly. 'What a dreadful thing for anyone to say. I want to know who said it.'

'I can't tell you that. But the same person alleges that at the time, a soldier called Mortimer—whose name, you'll remember, Boley linked with yours—was your boyfriend.'

'He wasn't,' she snapped. 'But what if he was?'

'If he was, and if Boley *had* attacked you, he would have had an overwhelming reason to go after Boley and mete out his own punishment, wouldn't he?'

Scobie was sure the brief smile that flickered across her face was one of relief, not amusement.

'Well, yes, I suppose he would . . . if any of this were true . . . which it isn't.' She had regained her composure. 'Someone has been telling you fairy tales, Chief Inspector.'

'That was not my impression,' Millson said tartly. 'Do you know why Sergeant Boley was discharged from the army?'

'No, you asked me that when you were here before. And I told you there's no reason why I should.'

'You were a nursing orderly in sick bay, were you not?'

'Ye-es.' Her tone was suddenly wary.

'Sergeant Boley was attacked during the night exercise . . . viciously attacked. He would have been admitted to sick bay, I imagine.'

'If he was, I don't recall it.'

'His injuries were of a nature that would have aroused considerable comment.'

'Really? What were they?'

'He was neutered, Miss Jones. Deliberately.'

She said calmly, 'How unfortunate for him.'

'You don't sound very sympathetic,' Millson said.

'Chief Inspector, I work in a hospital. I'm the ward sister in a male surgical ward and I see and hear a great many things most people prefer not to speak about. You have told me of an event which happened many years ago to a man I didn't know. I don't see why you expect me to show sympathy.'

'Very well.' Millson sounded chastened. 'But you do see

that if my information is correct, it would explain why your and Mortimer's names are linked in Boley's notebook? Boley was hunting the man who did that to him and he believed the motive for it was what he'd done to you.'

'Yes, I see that. But as I've already said, your information doesn't happen to be correct.'

'Can you suggest any other reason for your name being in that notebook?'

'No, I can't. I told you so when you asked me before.'

'So you did.' Frustrated by her answers, Millson changed direction. 'Have you ever been married, Miss Jones?'

'Yes.' She snapped the word at him.

Millson waited and when she remained silent he cast his eyes round the room. 'I take it your husband doesn't live here?'

'We're divorced.'

'When was that?'

She raised her eyebrows. 'About fifteen years ago. We didn't get on together . . . and he didn't like the hours I kept. Policemen's wives have the same problem, I believe. I'm surprised you're interested. Would you like to see my *decree nisi*?' Her tone was caustic.

Millson was unperturbed. 'No, that won't be necessary. Any children?' he asked casually.

Glancing up from his notebook, Scobie saw her face crumple. She averted her head and stared at the floor.

'No,' she said quietly. 'I wasn't able to have children.'

'I'm sorry,' Millson said. 'I didn't mean to pry.' He'd been probing for a weak spot to break through her barrier of confidence and wasn't proud of the way he'd succeeded. 'I'm sorry,' he repeated.

Her head lifted. 'It's all right,' she said, 'I knew it when I married. I've known since . . .' Her voice faltered. 'Since I was quite young,' she ended.

She rose from her chair and went to the window, where

she stood gazing out into the garden. After a moment she said, 'One learns to live with these things.'

Scobie wondered if there was any significance in her saying 'these things' instead of 'a thing like that'.

'Well, one of them has to be lying,' Millson said in exasperation as he drove away. 'Which do you reckon, Norris? Shand or Miss Jones?'

'I'd say Shand,' Scobie said. 'I think he came out with that story about rape to sidetrack us. There'd be no reason for her to deny it if it were true. And she doesn't strike me as the sort of woman who'd be too embarrassed to speak about it.'

'I agree. But she might keep quiet to protect someone . . . this man Mortimer, for instance. Any luck with finding his address?'

'No. It's a fairly common name.'

'So's Shand.'

'Ah, we were lucky there. We knew his first name— White gave it to me. And the DSS had a recent address for him.'

'What about that check I asked for on the old cases of unsolved murders and unidentified bodies?' Millson asked.

'There are none that match Boley's case.'

Boley's hunt for his attacker had begun with Colin White. White, manning a Bren gun post, had been the man nearest to Boley's position—a mere hundred yards away. It would have been a simple matter in the dark for him to leave his post, attack Boley, and return without being noticed. And he was a prime suspect for another reason.

The night before the exercise, Boley had caught a WRAC and a soldier together in a deserted area of the barracks that was out-of-bounds to troops. He'd been too interested in the girl to take much notice of the man and had ordered him back to quarters without bothering to identify him.

Moments later, as Boley forced himself on a terrified Ruth Jones, he was interrupted by the soldier who, hearing her cries, had returned to rescue her. Enraged, Boley drew his truncheon and felled the man. Leaving him unconscious on the ground, he caught up with the fleeing girl and continued the assault.

Boley considered the unidentified soldier to be the most likely person to have attacked him—taking revenge because he was the girl's lover. Boley had made discreet inquiries about Ruth's boyfriends and been given the names of White and Mortimer. Both of them had been near enough to him in the exercise to carry out the attack. They became his chief suspects, followed by a Corporal Tilley—whose wife Boley had made free with after a mess party a month ago —and Eric Shand.

Boley believed he would know when he'd found his man. One look into the eyes would tell him. When he arrived at White's house the man greeted him awkwardly, but Boley saw no hint of guilt or fear in his face. Boley told him he was investigating an accident that had occurred during the night exercise two months ago. He pulled out the map he'd made and cross-examined White on what he was doing at the time of the attack. White answered his questions readily and when Boley asked if he knew Ruth Jones, he laughed.

'You mean intimately? I should be so lucky!'

Boley nodded. Anyway, White was too short. The man he'd beaten to the ground in the dark was taller than White.

'What about Mortimer?' he asked.

White nodded. 'Yes, he went around with her.'

Wilfred Mortimer lived in London with his parents. They were out when Boley called in. He felt a surge of anticipation as Mortimer invited him in and offered him a drink. This man was exactly the right height and build and a searching stare into the eyes had caused him to look away nervously. Also he seemed over-friendly to Boley's suspicious mind.

As they engaged in small talk about the army over a glass of sherry, Boley inserted his question and watched Mortimer's reaction.

'You had a girlfriend it the Garrison, I remember. Ruth Jones, wasn't it?'

Mortimer's face was blank. 'Ruth? She wasn't my girlfriend. I hardly knew her.'

'Someone told me you was right close, you two. Lovebirds, they said.'

'I can't think why anyone would say that.' Mortimer looked uncomfortable.

Boley's lids hooded his eyes. The man was lying, of course. 'I 'spect you knows why I'm here . . . what I'm investigating.'

'No, I've no idea, Sergeant.'

'Not a sergeant any longer,' Boley rumbled. 'Bin discharged. Medical reasons,' he added meaningfully.

'Oh, I'm sorry to hear that.'

Boley's hard blue eyes bored into Wilfred Mortimer's face. 'A man was attacked . . . savagely attacked . . . in a night exercise you was on. That's what I's investigating . . . an' I'm gonna nail the man who done it.'

He took out his map, opened it on his lap and began questioning Mortimer. Like White, Mortimer had been manning a fixed position, only a field away from Boley.

'Did you leave your position during the exercise?' he demanded.

'No.'

'You could've slipped away for a bit and no one would have known.'

Neither would anyone have known he hadn't. Mortimer's face creased with apprehension.

'Say, between 0200 and 0230?' Boley pressed.

'No. I didn't leave my post,' Mortimer said, his voice

rising. 'Our instructions were to stay put until we received the order to advance.'

Boley's voice became dangerously quiet. 'You see, son, this man must've come from where you was and I reckon you's the one I'm looking for.' His eyes opened wide and blazed at Mortimer.

Mortimer shied away from the maniacal glare and seeing the fear in his face, Boley smiled maliciously. He'd found his man. It wouldn't take long to beat a confession out of him. And then . . . Boley's thick fingers clenched in expectation.

'Ain't no one else,' he continued remorselessly, ''less maybe you saw another soldier come by, eh?'

Mortimer shook his head. 'Only one of the instructors. He crawled past me in the dark. I don't think he saw me because I kept dead still and didn't give myself away. I assumed he was the enemy, you see.'

Boley's smile became sardonic. Crafty devil thought he could invent another suspect, did he? Because of the expertise needed to approach his position undetected, attack him and melt away again, Boley had checked and cross-checked every instructor's movements during the exercise, using logbooks, notes and message reports. He'd satisfactorily accounted for them all, apart from Corporal Tilley.

He decided to let Mortimer wriggle a while longer and tie himself in knots with his own lies. 'Tell me more 'bout this man,' he said softly. 'Why's you think he was an instructor?'

'Because he wasn't wearing full kit like the rest of us, only denims and a balaclava.'

'Yeh?' Boley's mouth twisted sceptically.

Anxiously, Wilfred tried to recall other details. 'And there was something else,' he said, remembering. 'His balaclava caught on a branch and almost came off as he crawled through the hedge. His face was blackened but his head was white—I saw it quite distinctly, even in the dark.

Funny that, now I come to think of it. An instructor with white hair.'

Boley was about to snarl his disbelief when understanding burst on him like a thunderclap. He went rigid with shock. White showing in the darkness. Not hair. *Bandages.* Mortimer wasn't lying after all. Mortimer wasn't his man . . . nor Shand . . . nor Corporal Tilley. The man who'd savaged him that night hadn't even been in the exercise. He'd come from the hospital. It was the man who'd fought with him over Ruth Jones in the darkness of a barracks wall, the man he'd beaten to the ground with his truncheon.

He saw it all now. Ruth Jones taking her injured lover to sick bay. Booking him in—a nameless statistic in next morning's parade state. Then covering for him when he slipped out of sick bay that night . . . She'd *colluded* . . . known what he was going to do.

Boley's rage flared into insanity. He'd soon find out who the man was. As soon as he laid hands on Ruth Jones again.

On his day off, Scobie usually met Kathy Benson for a drink in the Black Dog in Tanniford. Today, however, they'd met at the yacht club in Walton-on-the-Naze where Kathy was a member.

They sat on the small verandah overlooking the quay. It was a hot July day and Kathy was in a white summer dress and white, open-toed sandals. Norris Scobie wore a suit and was regretting it.

The tide was up and a dinghy race was under way. As they watched the boats tacking back and forth, Kathy said wistfully, 'I wish I still had a boat. I learned to sail here, you know.'

'Uh-huh.' Scobie was only half-listening. His eye had been caught by the sleek green hull of a vessel lying alongside the quay. 'That's *Moon Dancer*, Max Douglas's boat,' he said.

Kathy turned her head. 'Not now it isn't. He sold it after the accident. The club secretary bought it.'

'Yes, well, he wouldn't want to keep it in the circumstances, I suppose.'

'I don't think the accident was the reason he sold it,' Kathy said. 'He didn't need it any more.'

Scobie frowned. 'What are you getting at, Kathy?'

'I've heard he used it as a love-nest.' She smiled impishly. 'A *floating* love-nest. Apparently, he brought his girlfriends down from London, spent the day on board drinking and what have you and then took them home again. Cheaper than a hotel, I imagine.'

'Was this just rumour? Or is it true?' Scobie asked with sudden interest.

'Why?' Kathy smirked. 'Not getting ideas are you, Norris? I thought you liked my flat?'

He gave an easy laugh and shook his head. 'Just curious. Douglas gave us the line that he and his wife were very happy together.'

'Ah-hah. You mean, you're not sure his wife's death *was* an accident?'

'Kathy,' Scobie said severely, 'you know I—'

'Never discuss cases. Yes, I know. Would you if we were married?' she asked in a teasing voice.

'Why don't you marry me and find out?'

Her eyebrows came together in a frown. It was a point of friction between them. They'd known each other a year and Norris Scobie was eager to marry. Kathy was not. 'Most of the people I know have ended up separated, divorced, or thoroughly miserable,' she'd told him. Like George Millson, Scobie thought gloomily.

'You *know* why,' Kathy said, giving his hand a reassuring squeeze. 'Now . . . if you really want to know about Max Douglas and *Moon Dancer* ask one of the watermen. They'll tell you.'

'OK. Where do I find them?'

Kathy shaded her eyes against the sun and gazed towards the boatyard. 'There's one now.' She pointed to a figure in blue overalls on the deck of a Dutch *Boeier*.

Scobie put down his beer glass. 'Won't be a moment then.' He descended the verandah steps and strolled along the quay to where the *Boeier* was moored.

The boatman was reeving a new halyard through a mast-head pulley. He paused to eye Scobie warily as he stepped aboard in collar and tie and business suit.

'Police.' Scobie showed his warrant card. 'Mind if I ask you about the cruiser moored along the quay there?'

The man squinted towards *Moon Dancer*. 'What about her?'

'Tell me about her last owner.'

The man's suntanned face was impassive. 'What like?'

'I hear he was a bit of a lad with the girls.'

'Oh . . . that.' The man pulled on the reeving line, hauling one end of the halyard to the top of the mast, through the pulley and down again. 'Moored in the yacht basin then, she was. He'd drive up there with a girl and they'd go aboard. Then a bit later . . .' The boatman smiled a knowing smile and swayed his hips from side to side. 'The Rocking Boat, us used to call her.'

'Did he ever bring his wife?'

'Not until recent. They wen' out several times together this year. Reckon she put a stop to his goings-on after this dick come nosing around 'an told her what hubby was up to.'

Scobie pricked up his ears. 'A private detective?'

'Yeh, nice bloke. Very civil, he was.'

Which Scobie interpreted as meaning he'd paid the boatman for information. 'How long ago was this?'

The brown forehead creased in thought. 'Near enough a twelvemonth, I reckon.'

'You don't happen to remember his name or where he came from?'

'Yeh. He come from Colchester an' he were called Harvey.' The man sniggered. 'First name were Dick.'

Ruth Jones no longer lived-in at the barracks, Boley discovered. She had a small basement flat at the Hythe. The day after his visit to Wilfred Mortimer, he obtained the address over the phone from the orderly room and took the train to Colchester that evening.

Ruth had just come off duty and was in her khaki uniform when she opened the door to him. She blanched as she saw him standing there and tried to close the door in his face, but he blocked it with his boot.

'You scream an' it'll be your last!' he snarled, forcing his way in and kicking the door to behind him. 'I want answers —an' fast!'

'Wha-what about?'

'Who is he?'

She said bravely, 'I don't know what you mean.'

'Don't mess me about!' Without warning he slammed his fist into her abdomen.

She doubled up, gasping and retching. 'You can't do this to me!'

He seized her by the hair, pulled her head up and thrust his face into hers. 'I'll do what I like to you, you Welsh tart! Now, I want the name of the guy you was with that night. Regular boyfriend, was he?'

'No . . . I'd never seen him before.'

'You's lying! After I'd finished with you, you went back an' found him. Took him to sick bay, didn't you? Now who was he?' He drew back his arm.

'No, please! Don't hit me there. I'm—'

His fist drove into her again and she sank to her knees sobbing with pain.

'His name! I want his name!' Boley howled. He lifted her by her collar like a rag doll and as she looked up into the merciless eyes he raised his fist yet again.

'*No!*' she screamed and babbled the name.

'Where is he now?'

'I don't know. He wouldn't touch me after what you did. *I don't!*' she shrieked as she saw his fist rising. 'I'd tell you if I did.'

'No matter, I'll find him.' Boley released her and she collapsed in a heap on the floor.

She'd gained a little time. Time enough, she hoped, to reach the man before Boley did and warn him.

CHAPTER 12

The morning after his day off with Kathy, Scobie found Millson in an irritable mood again, this time because of a further call from his solicitor warning him of an impending visit by court welfare officers.

'The court requires a report on you and on your daughter's home environment,' the solicitor had told him. 'So make sure the house is squeaky clean. And above all, be nice to them. *Crawl*, if you have to. Forget you're a policeman. You're a loving dad whose daughter is the apple of his eye and you'll do anything they want to keep her with you. Understand?'

Millson glowered at Scobie as he reported Max Douglas's carryings-on aboard *Moon Dancer*. 'What were you doing wasting time on that?'

Scobie bridled. 'I didn't *waste* time. It was my day off and I happened to be at the yacht club with Kathy.'

'In that case I should have thought you'd have something better to do with your time,' Millson said acidly. 'Douglas's affairs with these girls might conceivably be a motive for his wife to kill *him*. They are certainly not a reason for him to kill *her*.'

'There's rather more to it than that.' Following his talk

with the waterman, Scobie had spoken to the club secretary, who knew Max Douglas well. 'Douglas has sold up and gone off to Spain with a girl called Poppy.'

'Did he know this girl before his wife's accident?'

'He must have done because he went off with her right after the funeral. Suppose he'd wanted a divorce so's he could be with this girl and his wife wouldn't give him one? That'd be a motive to get rid of her.'

Millson sighed wearily. 'All right, Norris. No one shall say we left any stones unturned. Dig out the inquiry agent and find out what Mrs Douglas did about his report and whether he can tell you anything about this Poppy.'

Poppy Latimer was in a quandary. Two days ago a removal van had delivered everything Max had put in store when he sold his London house. He'd spent yesterday sorting out correspondence and files, selecting and discarding and filling several bins.

This morning when he was out, Poppy had gone through everything, including the material he'd thrown away. In the dustbin she found the stubs of several used cheque-books. One of them had been Daphne's. Poppy went carefully through the counterfoils and came to one that made her eyes gleam in triumph. *P.L.: £2000.* It was the counter-foil of the cheque Daphne had made out to her and which Max said he hadn't found. She looked at the date. It was two days before Daphne's accident.

She stared angrily at the slip of paper. This was the advance Auntie D. had promised her, the money that would have enabled her to leave home. Daphne *had* written the cheque before she died. That slob Max had lied to her! He must have found the cheque and destroyed it.

Encouraged by the discovery she continued searching. She had found nothing more, however, nothing to show Auntie D. had intended setting up a trust fund for her.

Now, disheartened, she had to decide what to do. If she

challenged him with the cheque stub he'd only say Daphne must have changed her mind and torn the cheque up. So, what now?

She contemplated the choices. Go back home? She shuddered. That wasn't even a starter. Go it alone? No, she'd had enough of scrimping and scraping. What then? It was time to think the unthinkable: to consider *marrying* Max Douglas. After all, she was already engaged to him.

Could she go through with it? She could look upon what she'd endured so far as an investment . . . a deposit. Pay the balance and the goods would be hers. One thing the search had revealed, as she ploughed through share certificates and bank statements, was that Max Douglas was a great deal wealthier than she'd realized. He was what her stepfather called 'stinking rich'.

Yes, she could do it. It wouldn't be for long, she told herself. She didn't intend to stay with him. Once she'd talked him into a joint bank account, credit accounts at Harrods and the other big stores and persuaded him to part with the rest of Auntie D.'s jewellery, she'd be ready to leave. She'd drain the accounts and be off. He'd lied to her and cheated. She'd take him for every penny she could . . . strip the creep to his underpants. That's what she'd do.

An inquiry by telephone to the orderly room in Colchester Garrison had given Boley the address of the man whose name he'd forced from Ruth Jones. Equipped with binoculars, sandwiches and Thermos flask, he spent two days and two nights in reconnaissance of the location and observing his quarry's movements and routine. Then he returned to Tanniford and planned his revenge.

''Bye, darling. See you tomorrow.' Outside Holly Cottage a girl wound up her car window and drove off into the night.

Boley's shadow glided from a hiding-place in the hedge,

indistinguishable from other shadows with its blackened face and dark combat clothes, and watched her rear-lights disappear round a bend in the lane. He'd chosen a moonless night—the first night of a new moon—and the sky was a velvet black sprinkled with the silver dots of distant stars.

Inside the cottage, twenty-year-old Max Douglas bolted the front door behind his guest, a local farmer's daughter, and returned to the sitting-room. He'd inherited the cottage at Duke's Green on the death of his mother. His father—a Guards officer—had been killed in the War. Selecting a book from a shelf, Max settled down in an armchair to read. Outside it was dark and silent.

A while later, there was a noise in the garden. Max stopped reading and listened. After his two years of National Service, he'd adapted to a rural life and invested in some chickens. The noise sounded like clucking in the hen-house at the bottom of the back garden and he wondered if there was a fox around. Suddenly there was a squawking and a flapping of wings. Max leapt from his chair and, grabbing a torch on his way through the kitchen, ran out of the back door and down the path.

The squawking sounds were coming from behind the hen-house and he ran round to the rear, shining the torch. As the beam lit up the wall of the shed he started back with shock. A flapping chicken hung by one leg, tethered by its claw to a hook on the wall. The bird's wing had been broken and it was in distress. Max stepped forward and quickly broke its neck, then untied the carcass and slipped the cord into his pocket.

He peered around him, holding the dead bird. Suddenly, the lights in the cottage went out. He dropped the bird and directed the torch beam at the back door. It was closed. He'd left it open.

Boley dropped to his knees behind a coal bunker as Max Douglas played the spotlight back and forth over the rear of the building. In his reconnaissance of the cottage and its surroundings Boley had studied the layout and memorized every feature. While Douglas had been out in the garden, he'd entered the cottage through the back door. Bolting it behind him, he'd flicked up the mains switch on the electric meter in the kitchen, let himself out of the front door and doubled back to the rear again. The garden was now in darkness and Douglas couldn't get back into the house. He'd deliberately lured his quarry into the darkness and cut off his retreat in order to prolong his revenge. Boley burned with sadistic hate. He intended his victim to suffer for a while, agonizing over what would happen to him when he was caught.

'Douglas? This is Boley!' His voice boomed into the blackness.

Max stood immobilized with shock for a moment, then swung the torch in the direction of the voice. But Boley had already moved. Max recovered himself, switched off the torch and dropped to the ground.

'What do you want?' He raised his head, listening for the direction of the reply.

There was a sudden noise close by. Instinctively he rolled over and away from it and leapt to his feet, losing the torch as he did so. Boley's voice came from a different direction and Max realized he'd used the trick of throwing a stone to distract him while he changed his position.

'You know why I'm here,' Boley called.

'No, I don't. Stop playing games.'

Boley's voice dripped malice. 'It ain't no game, Douglas. I'm gonna mangle you . . . like you done me.'

'It wasn't me, I swear it!'

'Don't waste breath lying. You was *seen*, Douglas . . . crawling along, your head bandaged. An' I talked to your tart, Ruth Jones. I beat your name outta her.'

Max shrivelled inside. Those frantic messages to his office yesterday to ring her . . . messages he'd ignored because he didn't want to renew their association . . .

'Listen, you're making a mistake!' he shouted. 'It wasn't me—'

'Longer you whine, son, longer this'll take.' Boley sniggered. 'But I's not in any hurry.'

Max felt an emptiness in the pit of his stomach. Boley could have overpowered and crippled him when he first came out, unsuspecting, into the dark. Instead, the fiend intended to drag things out in some kind of macabre manhunt. Max assessed his chances of escaping across the open fields. Boley would have considered that possibility and either decided he couldn't make it, or devised a means to prevent him. Besides, it was no use running away. Boley would only come after him another time. There'd be a push from behind on a crowded Underground platform . . . or petrol through the letter-box, torching the cottage and him with it . . . No, he'd have no peace of mind until this ogre was dealt with.

'Thinking, are you, Douglas?' Boley's voice whispered through the night.

Max began to crawl quietly over the grass.

Boley's voice came again. 'Lost your tongue? That ain't all you're gonna lose.' There was a coarse laugh. 'Jes' you an' me, Douglas . . . in the dark. Cosy, in't it?'

Keep talking, Max breathed, creeping forward in the direction of the voice.

A moment later Boley called from another direction, taunting him. 'Yer face is white as a baby's bum and you's going the wrong way.'

Cursing under his breath, Max jumped up and ran to the side of the garden, away from the voice. He hurled himself through the hedge and dropped down into the ditch beyond. Clawing up mud, he smothered his face and then rolled around in the ditch to camouflage his clothing.

Lying there, he summoned up the skills he'd learned— some from Boley himself—during that three-week course. Turning his cheek slowly from side to side, he checked the movement of the night air. He was upwind of Boley and, for all his camouflage, the scent of his aftershave and haircream could betray him. He must get downwind of the man. Where exactly was he, though?

Max tried to trick him into giving away his position. 'You'll get prison for it, you know, Boley!' he shouted.

There was no reply and he had the unnerving fear his enemy was close by, about to pounce. Then from somewhere near the vegetable patch, Boley's voice floated into the gloom.

'Not after what you done to me, I won't. An' anyways, it'll be worth it.'

Max began moving quietly down the hedge to the weatherboard fence across the bottom of the garden. The tall fence would provide cover to the other side of the garden from where he could work his way up towards Boley from downwind.

He reached the cover of the fence and stood up. Moving swiftly, he followed the fence, pausing every few steps to listen. The only sounds were the natural noises of the night.

He came to the end of the fence and turned the corner. Suddenly a shadow reared up under his feet with a snarl of triumph. Boley's arm encircled him, hugging his body tight against his own to pin his arms.

'Nice silhouette you made 'gainst the night sky,' Boley rasped. 'You's forgotten what I taught you.'

His free hand gripped Max's throat, thumb and forefinger either side digging viciously into the carotid arteries.

Max felt his senses slipping as the blood supply to his brain was cut off. In a few seconds he would black out and Boley would exact a ghastly revenge. As a last desperate resort he went limp, feigning unconsciousness. Taken by surprise at the sudden dead weight, Boley's hold slackened. Max jerked free, threw himself sideways in a running roll and leapt away into the darkness. Racing up the garden, he flung himself to the ground behind the garage and put his hands over his mouth to muffle his ragged breathing.

When his breathing quietened he sat up and fingered his bruised neck. There was only one way to stop Boley now. Max took the length of cord the chicken had been tied with from his pocket. He made a wide loop, twisted it and doubled it under to form the second loop of a constrictor knot. The constrictor was a sailor's knot, a self-tightening, non-slip knot for securing a cord to a round object like an oar or a bollard. It was a complicated knot to form in the dark, but Max had had plenty of practice with the Sea Scouts.

He crept along the side of the garage to the doors at the front. Gently, he pulled one ajar so that it made a slight noise. Enough to catch Boley's keen ears, but not so loud he would suspect a trap. Then he melted into the shadows of the nearby hedge and knelt on one knee.

The smell of Boley's sweat reached him first. Then he detected his dark outline moving, almost imperceptibly, along the garage wall. It seemed an age before Boley reached the front corner of the garage and stood motionless behind the open door, listening.

Max came silently to his feet, holding the loops carefully between his hands. He would have only the one chance. He took two quick steps, dropped the double noose over Boley's head and jerked the ends of the cord in opposite directions to close the loops and operate the deadly self-tightening knot.

Boley whirled round, clawing at the cords biting into his neck. Max stepped back. Boley was doomed. The more he struggled the harder the knot would tighten and the deeper the ligatures would cut into his neck.

Impassively, he watched Boley sink to his knees, fingernails tearing at the thin cord, then topple over, gagging and choking.

Fifteen seconds later he was dead.

CHAPTER 13

The morning after he killed Boley, Max Douglas received a frantic phone call from Ruth Jones at his office. She'd been trying to reach him for three days. Hadn't he received her messages? she asked. He had, but he'd thought she was trying to renew their relationship and hadn't called her back.

'I've been out a lot,' he lied.

'Well, thank God I've reached you now.' She told him of Boley's visit and the beating he'd given her. 'He's insane, Max . . . utterly mad. I had to give him your name —' She caught her breath. 'I think he would have killed me if I hadn't. I didn't tell him where you lived, though. Max . . . I'm sorry . . .'

For a fleeting moment, he was ready to tell her Boley was dead. Then caution intervened and he comforted her instead.

'It's all right, Ruth. You've nothing to be sorry for. It's my fault what's happened.'

'But he's bound to find you and —'

'Don't worry about it. I'm forewarned, thanks to you. I can take care of myself. Have you told anyone else he's after me?'

'No, of course not.'

'Good girl. Then don't, please.'

'Max . . . ?'

'Yes?'

She hesitated over whether to tell him. 'Nothing. Take care . . . 'bye.'

'Goodbye, Ruth.'

Ruth Jones was friendly with several soldiers at the time she met Max Douglas. He was handsome and charming and quite different from the other men she'd known. She fell for him instantly. Her affair with him was short-lived, however—brought to an end before anyone else was aware of it by Boley's defilement of her.

As they helped each other to the Casualty Department that evening, Max swore vengeance on Boley. Not only for what he'd done to Ruth, but for Max's own dishonour and guilt. He'd failed to protect her; his manhood was in question.

Neither of them reported Boley. Ruth went straight back on duty at the hospital and Max, to explain his injuries, told the medical staff he'd fallen down an iron staircase. His wounds were dressed and he was admitted to sick bay with suspected concussion.

The following evening, after the troops had departed for the night exercise, Max slipped out of sick bay with Ruth's connivance and obtained the location of Boley's post from the exercise map on the wall of the instructors' room.

Later that night, dressed in combat clothes and equipped with a night compass, he cycled to the exercise site at Fing-ringhoe on Ruth's bike. He hid the bike in undergrowth and in the darkness and the confusion of troops, moved undetected through the lines to where Boley lay. Then, coldly and brutally, he savaged him.

When Max re-entered sick bay in the small hours of the morning, no one except Ruth knew he'd ever left there.

The day after a local newspaper reported Boley's disappearance, Max received a letter from Ruth Jones enclosing the cutting from the paper. Although she was not explicit, it was clear from the way she referred to Boley never troubling either of them again, that she realized he was dead and that Max had killed him. 'Boley was a mad beast who deserved to die,' she wrote.

The letter bade Max a loving farewell, acknowledging

their love-affair could never be rekindled. Then, at the very end of the letter, Ruth told him of the final tragedy Boley had brought on her . . . on them both.

As he read the letter, Max realized that what Ruth had written incriminated her and made her an accessory to Boley's murder. He was a realist. If he were questioned, he needed Ruth's alibi for the night of the exercise. And if he were charged with killing Boley, her testimony would be vital in support of pleas of self-defence and extreme provocation. He was confident that with her evidence a jury would acquit him of murder. The letter would serve to remind Ruth—if he ever had to—that she'd made herself an accessory to murder and must cooperate with him. He locked the letter and newspaper report away safely, in case he ever needed them.

Max thought it unlikely Boley would have told anyone he was coming to Duke's Green. If he was asked he would say Boley called to talk over their time together in the army, they had a few drinks and then he left. No one could prove otherwise. Only one person would know the real reason for Boley's visit . . . that he would never have dropped in for a chat. And she would never tell.

Over the next few weeks there was a report of an interview with Boley's mother in one newspaper and short paragraphs about his disappearance in two others. After that, nothing. No one called on Max to inquire about Boley and as the weeks and then the months passed, he knew no one ever would. He was safe. He dismissed Boley from his mind and continued with his life.

Scobie found the address of the inquiry agent, Richard Harvey, in Yellow Pages. The office was above a shop in a run-down part of the town near the Hythe. Richard Harvey was a fat, scruffily-dressed man who chain-smoked. Years of heavy smoking had taken their toll. The whites of his watery eyes were an unhealthy yellow and every now and again he succumbed to a bout of bronchial coughing.

When Scobie announced himself and showed his warrant card, Harvey gave him an ingratiating smile and commented that he was in the same line of business, so to speak. Scobie let it pass.

'I understand you undertook some inquiries for a Mrs Douglas about a year ago?'

'Douglas? . . . Douglas? Don't recall her. Matrimonial?'

'I imagine so. Memory not very good?' Scobie asked, irritated by Harvey's offhand manner.

'Nothing wrong with my memory. Just very busy with a lot of cases, that's all. The population bulge after the War, you know. In their forties now. And that's the peak time for marriages to pack up. What's her first name?'

'Daphne.'

'Right . . .' Harvey turned to a computer screen on his desk and pecked at the keyboard with his fingers. 'Here we are. Yes, she was a client of mine.' He swivelled his revolving chair to a chest of filing cabinets and pulled out a drawer. Flicking through the hanging files, he extracted one and laid it on his desk. 'What's your interest?'

'Just routine.'

Harvey patted the folder with his hand. 'My inquiries are confidential.'

'Like hell they are!' Scobie snapped. He pulled out his notebook. 'This is in connection with a murder inquiry and I want information.'

Harvey sniffed, pulled a grey-white handkerchief from his pocket and wiped his nose. 'Ah well, in that case . . .' He opened the folder and glanced at the top sheet. 'She asked me to check on her old man.' He turned the page over and scanned the typewritten sheets beneath, nodding his head. 'Oh yes . . . I remember *him*. He was having it off on his motor-cruiser . . . more comfortable than the back of the car, I guess. Lovely craft . . . I took a peek through

the windows. A floating motel. Beautifully fitted out . . .
double bunks . . . carpets . . . drinks bar. Some guys have
it made, don't they?' He leered at Scobie.

'Why did Mrs Douglas choose *you*?' Scobie asked, with
deliberate contempt to wipe the leer off the man's face. 'Why
not a London agent? They lived in Wimbledon, didn't they?'

The leer remained and Harvey's mouth opened in a grin
of nicotine-stained teeth. 'Ah, but you see they own a
country cottage down here at Duke's Green and wifey
thought that's where hubby was getting up to his tricks. So
she wanted a local man. Mind you, she wan't that far wrong
'cos, like I said, he was using his boat at Walton. Probably
thought he was safer there than the cottage.'

Harvey lit a fresh cigarette from the end of the one he
was smoking and ground the stub in an ashtray. 'Anyway,
I kept tabs on him for about six weeks—followed the girls
when he took 'em home and so on—and then I wrote up
my report and gave it to Mrs Douglas.'

'What was her reaction?'

'Hopping mad, she was. I don't think she'd any idea he
was involved with so many girls. You should have seen her
face when she read the report.'

'She didn't bring divorce proceedings, though?'

'No. Not so far as I know.'

'These girls Mr Douglas was seeing . . . was there one
called Poppy?'

Harvey picked up the typewritten pages and scanned
them. 'Tracey . . . Debby . . . Mia . . . No, there's no
Poppy.' He dropped the pages and looked up with a frown.
'Poppy. Wait a minute . . .' He swivelled his chair and
attacked the keyboard again, his eyes on the screen. Suddenly he clicked his tongue. 'Told you there's nothing
wrong with my memory,' he said, giving Scobie an accusing
glare. 'Mrs Douglas asked me to trace a girl called Poppy.'

Scobie's interest quickened. 'When was this?'

'Hang on.' Harvey swivelled the other way and delved

in the filing cabinet again. He pulled out another folder and opened it on his desk. He read for a moment then said, 'April . . . four months ago. It took me a couple of months to find her. Name of Latimer. She was seventeen . . . maybe eighteen . . . working in Putney.'

'Why did Mrs Douglas want to find her?'

'Search me. She never said. Could have been a relative, I suppose. Anyway, the girl wasn't anything to do with her old man. Poppy wasn't one of his popsies.' Yellow teeth parted in another grin at the joke. 'Mrs D. was very friendly with her.'

'So Mrs Douglas *met* Poppy Latimer?'

'Oh yes. She asked me to arrange the meeting. That was the last I heard.'

'Douglas lied to us about his happy relationship with his wife,' Scobie told Millson in the office that afternoon. 'He was a regular Casanova, according to the inquiry agent. He was carrying on with a number of girls and his wife was furious when she found out.'

'What did she do about it?'

'He doesn't know. Perhaps she threatened to divorce him unless he behaved. The boatman at the yacht club said Douglas stopped bringing girls to the boat and began taking his wife out instead.'

'So you reckon he reformed?' Millson said.

'Not necessarily. I think maybe he was just biding his time to get rid of her. She was nearly fifty, remember, and he had a penchant for young girls.'

'So do most middle-aged men, Norris. It's a longing that comes with age. It's not a motive for murder. It's not even half a motive. If a man like Douglas wanted to go off with a young girl he'd just leave his wife, he wouldn't murder her. A threat of divorce wouldn't bother him. What did you find out about this girl, Poppy?'

'She's something of a mystery. Her name's Poppy

Latimer and four months ago Daphne Douglas asked the
same inquiry agent to find the girl for her. She didn't say why
and when he found her, she asked him to arrange a meeting
with the girl. They were very friendly together, he says.'

Millson frowned. 'So Douglas *did* know the girl before his
wife's accident?'

'Presumably. Although the agent was certain he wasn't
having an affair with her.'

Millson grunted. 'Unless he was more discreet with her
than the others.' He pursed his lips. 'I don't think this gives
us a reason to question Douglas again, though.'

'No, I suppose not,' Scobie said reluctantly.

'Definitely not,' Millson said firmly. 'And it's time we
made some progress on the Boley case. Still no addresses
for the other two men, Mortimer and Tilley?'

Scobie shook his head. 'Doesn't look as though we're
going to find them.'

Millson sucked his teeth. 'We need more information. I'd
like to meet Boley's mother. There may be something she's
overlooked and it won't hurt to prod her memory. What's
she like?'

'Seems a nice old lady. I don't know how she could have
produced a monster like Boley.'

'We don't know he was a monster, Norris.'

'White and Shand said he was.'

'I'll bet his mother doesn't think so.'

Millson was right. 'Oh, he was a good lad, was Stanford
. . . a lovely boy,' Mrs Boley told him. 'No mother could
ask for better. A wonderful son. Luke here's the same.'

Scobie glanced sideways at the middle-aged Lucas sitting
beside her on the sofa as she reached out and patted his
hand. Lucas winked and gave her a loving smile. Scobie
was fond of his own mother, but he couldn't imagine himself
living at home or gawping at her the way Lucas Boley was
doing.

Emily Boley took a framed photograph from the mantelpiece and handed it to Millson. It was similar to the one
Scobie had taken away with him for the file. 'That's Stan,'
she said.

Millson examined it politely. Stanford Boley looked a
thug, there were no two ways about it. Not a man he'd care
to meet in a dark alley. However, Millson reminded himself
as he returned the picture to her, even thugs had a right
not to be murdered.

Mrs Boley replaced the photograph on the mantelpiece.
'You'll be wanting a cup of tea,' she said.

Scobie saw Millson about to refuse and said earnestly,
'Mrs Boley brews an excellent cup of tea, sir. You ought to
try it.'

Millson nodded. It would give him the opportunity to
speak to Lucas without his mother being present. 'Very
well. Thank you, Mrs Boley.'

She left the room and he turned to Lucas Boley. 'From
inquiries we've made we've discovered your brother was
discharged from the army on medical grounds.'

Lucas knew that. It said so in the letter he'd found with
Stan's papers in the loft and kept to himself. 'Well, don't
tell Ma that. She likes to remember Stan fit and healthy.'

'I've no intention of telling her,' Millson said. 'But I
think *you* should know what happened.'

He thought Lucas Boley might misunderstand clinical
terms or euphemisms, so he told him in plain language.

Lucas Boley's mouth dropped and then his eyes flamed
with a murderous rage, quickly veiled. Later, Millson wondered if he'd been wise to disclose the information.

'Who dome that to Stan?' Lucas demanded angrily.

'We don't know, but we think it was the man your
brother was looking for.'

'One of them in his notebook?'

'Probably. We need to find out which of them he went
to see on the day he went missing.'

'Well, it's no good asking me. I was only a kid then. You'd best ask Ma.'

Mrs Boley returned with the tea-tray. 'We'll just let it draw a bit,' she said, setting it on a sidetable and sitting down beside Lucas on the sofa again.

'Mrs Boley, did your son mention any enemies . . . anyone who might have a grudge against him?' Millson asked.

Her forehead creased in concentration. 'No, not that I remember,' she said. 'He was a nice boy . . . everyone liked him.'

Scobie and Millson looked at each other, marvelling at the blindness of mother-love.

'You see,' Millson confided, 'we're at a bit of a dead end. Did he give any hint of who he was going to see, or where he was going that last day?'

She shook her head. Turning to the tea-tray, she lifted the pewter teapot and began pouring. 'No, I've thought and thought. This journalist woman asked the same thing.'

Millson's head jerked round. 'Journalist? What journalist?'

She handed him a teacup. 'Came here 'bout a year ago and said she was doing research on missing persons. She'd looked through old newspaper reports and seen about Stanford. She showed me the cutting.'

Scobie looked up from making notes. 'The actual newspaper cutting, Mrs Boley? Not a photocopy?'

'No, it were a piece of the newspaper.'

Scobie made a note. Journalists didn't usually carry around newspaper cuttings from thirty years ago. He heard Millson follow up the point.

'What paper was it from, do you remember, Mrs Boley?'

'The *Essex Standard*.'

'And the reporter's name?'

Her brow wrinkled. 'Smith . . . *Betty* Smith, I think she said.'

Although there were thousands, probably millions, of

people in the world called Smith, Millson always felt a twinge of suspicion when the name popped up unexpectedly in an investigation.

'Did she show you a Press card? Or say what paper she was from?'

'No. From the way she was talking, though, it were the *Essex Standard.*'

'What did she look like? Can you describe her for me?' Millson asked.

Mrs Boley thought for a moment. 'Fiftyish. Smart . . . good clothes. And blonde hair—though it come out of a bottle, I reckon.'

Millson was thoughtful as they drove away from Tanniford. The woman journalist—though he doubted if she was a journalist—had asked Mrs Boley several times whether she'd heard from her son since he disappeared. She had seemed more interested in that than in his disappearance.

'Who was she, Norris? And where the heck did she get an actual newspaper cutting of thirty years ago? Get round to the *Standard* offices and see what you can find out.'

CHAPTER 14

Driving away from Colchester in the red Mini that Max had bought her as an engagement present, Poppy Latimer negotiated the double roundabout on the by-pass and headed back to Duke's Green.

She hadn't seen anything she liked in the dress shops in the new shopping precinct. Perhaps she'd spend tomorrow in London's West End. If nothing else, it would provide a break from Max. She was finding it hard to keep up the pretence of being a loving fiancée. Harder still to tolerate his persistent caresses.

She'd taken advantage of this afternoon's shopping expedition to consult a solicitor without Max knowing. Giving the name of 'Mrs Green', she'd pretended to be married and insisted on paying the bill there and then. She wanted to find out how quickly she'd be able to get a divorce after she married Max and how she would stand financially.

The solicitor was a bald, middle-aged man with rubbery lips whose eyes burrowed under the hem of her skirt every time she crossed her legs. Without her husband's consent, he told her, she couldn't obtain a divorce for five years.

'What, not any way?' she asked, aghast.

'Not unless your husband was a naughty boy or beat you. Or if . . .'

Licking his lips, he started to explain the grosser activities that would entitle her to an earlier divorce if Max practised them upon her. Poppy cut him short and moved him on to money and assets.

'I take it you didn't bring any—er—assets into the matrimonial home with you?' the solicitor asked.

Any *other* assets that is, his eyes said, gazing lasciviously at her legs.

She shook her head. Could she keep everything she'd acquired? she asked. Anything that was an outright gift, yes. What about his first wife's jewellery? So far, Max had given her only a few items, but Poppy planned to take the lot. She was sure Auntie D. would have wanted her to.

The solicitor blew out his cheeks, Doubtful, unless her husband specifically gave it to her. How long had she been married? Poppy thought quickly and told him eight weeks —she thought that would be the limit of her endurance. 'Eight *weeks*?' His eyebrows shot up to where his hairline would have been if he'd had one. When they came down again the eyes had a knowing look. 'I *see*.'

He asked Max's age and gave her another knowing look when she told him. Children? Brothers or sisters of whole blood? No?

'Well, now . . .' The top of a tongue darted out between thick lips, slithered round them and disappeared into his mouth again. 'Bearing in mind your husband's—um . . . age and his financial circumstances . . .' He paused as Poppy recrossed her legs, his eyes hovering hopefully around her hemline. 'Is it wise to leave him just yet? Have you considered . . . ?'

He hummed and haw'd a lot but what he'd meant was that if she hung on, when Max died she'd scoop the lot, there being no other claimants. No, actually, she hadn't considered that because Max was healthy and virile. And because he intended to beget children—she hadn't grasped that until he began throwing out hints about it yesterday. *Kids!* Definitely not on her agenda. Neither was five years of marriage.

Poppy came to another roundabout and turned on to the Harwich road. She hadn't realized she wouldn't be able to get a divorce for five years. *Five years!* She stamped angrily on the accelerator. The mini's automatic gearbox changed down and the little red car screamed away from the roundabout like an angry bee.

Daphne Douglas had had difficulty delving into her husband's finances to discover whether or not he was dependent on her money. It was essential to find out, though, before she faced him with his misconduct and threatened to cut off his funds unless he behaved.

She needed to gain access to a deedbox where he kept his bank statements and other financial documents. The problem was that the key to it was on his key ring, which he always carried with him. Daphne was certain there would be a spare key hidden somewhere, but it took her a long time to find it. Eventually she discovered it taped to the underside of his desk, behind one of the drawers.

The next time Max was away from London for the day (Daphne shut her mind against the thought he was probably with a girl again) she took the key from its hiding-place and dragged the heavy metal box from the cupboard in his study. Unlocking it, she lifted out the bundles of papers, carefully laying them out in order on the carpet so that she could replace them exactly as they were. Then, with a notebook beside her on the floor, she went methodically through the bank statements, loan statements and share certificates, jotting down figures.

When she'd finished she stood up and poured herself a drink. Sitting down at his desk, she totted up the figures and made some calculations. She sat back with a satisfied smile. Max had a large overdraft secured against her own shares and guarantees. If she withdrew her support he'd be crippled, or badly hit at the very least.

She swallowed the rest of her drink and knelt down on the floor to begin replacing the papers in the box. As she put back the first batch of bank statements, she noticed a handwritten envelope lying at the bottom of the box. She picked it up. It was addressed to Max at Holly Cottage. An old love-letter, perhaps? Intrigued, Daphne opened the envelope and took out the letter inside.

As she began reading, her eyebrows contracted in a deep frown.

In her house in Tanniford, Emily Boley was in a flurry of activity. When she had called in at the estate agent's earlier, Kathy Benson had told her she had a definite buyer for her house. Emily was still unhappy at the thought of leaving her home, but she supposed Luke was right and she'd better get on with things, so she was energetically turning out cupboards and throwing away magazines and old news-papers.

Emily's house had open fireplaces and she had acquired the habit of saving paper—particularly newspaper—as a young girl. Her mother had taught her to make spills of tightly-twisted paper to light the fire with, saving the expense of buying firewood or firelighters. To this day, Emily lit her coal fires with paper. But Luke said their new place would have central heating, it wouldn't have fireplaces, so there was no point saving paper any more.

Emily trotted back and forth, depositing bundles of newspapers in the dustbin, the heavy type of the headlines occasionally catching her eye. DROWNING TRAGEDY AT STONE POINT slipped past her gaze like the other headlines, but the accompanying photograph registered subliminally. Seconds later Emily reached down into the bin and lifted the paper out again. Raising her spectacles from her nose, she peered with naked eye at the picture of the victim.

Clutching the paper, she shuffled to the telephone.

Scobie's inquiries at the offices of the various Essex newspapers drew blank. No one had heard of a journalist or reporter called Betty Smith and all the editors assured Scobie none of their staff had been engaged in research on missing persons a year ago.

Millson was in a strange mood when Scobie reported to him. Scobie wasn't sure if he was gloomy or cheerful. He seemed to be a mixture of both. The court had called to interview Millson and his daughter yesterday evening.

'Dena got very uptight with them,' Millson told Scobie. 'There was me . . . all milk and honey like the solicitor asked . . . and her—well, I've never seen her like that. She simply tore into them. Said they'd have to put her in a straitjacket to take her back to her mum. "You tell the judge that," she said. They started arguing with her.' Millson smiled ruefully. 'That was a mistake. She really lost her temper then. Told them to "bog off".' He shook his head wonderingly. '"Bog off", Norris. What sort of language is that for a twelve-year-old girl?'

'What happened?'

'They turned tail and went. I don't know whether I'm pleased or sorry.'

'What does your solicitor say?'

'I haven't dared tell him.'

It was midday when Scobie entered Millson's office the second time.

'You've got that look on your face again,' Millson complained. 'The "I know something you don't" look. What is it this time?'

'Guess who the journalist woman was who called on Mrs Boley?'

'I don't make guesses,' Millson said heavily. 'I deal in facts and I make deductions from facts. I may speculate— but that's not the same as guessing. Just tell me what you've found out.'

Scobie's mouth closed obstinately. Millson looked at him and sighed. 'All right, Norris,' he said patiently. 'Who was she?'

'Daphne Douglas,' Scobie said and was rewarded by seeing Millson's eyebrows rise sharply in twin arches. 'Mrs Boley's just been on the phone. She was turning out some old newspapers and came across a front page report of Daphne's drowning. There was a photograph with it and Mrs Boley recognized her. Quite definite, she is.'

Millson's face assumed a wolfish expression. 'Why on earth did Daphne Douglas pretend to be a newspaper reporter and ask questions about Stanford Boley? Did she know him? Or, more likely, did her husband know him?'

'Douglas is the right age to have been doing National Service with White and Shand. Shall I get on to MOD and check?'

'There's a quicker way, Norris. We'll ask Douglas himself. In fact, there are several things I want to ask him.' He leaned forward in his seat, rubbing his hands together between his knees. 'I knew there was something odd about his wife's death.'

'I thought I was the one who didn't believe it was an accident,' Scobie reminded him.

'Yes, but *you* thought the motive was sex or money. I told you it wasn't. If Douglas did kill his wife, it wasn't over another woman. There would have to be another reason— and a mighty strong one—to make him commit murder.'

'But his wife's visit to Mrs Boley was over a year ago.'

'If you want to murder your wife and get away with it, Norris,' Millson said, 'you don't kill her in the heat of the moment. You wait . . . you plan . . . and when the opportunity comes along to make it look like an accident —*that's* when you kill her.'

Millson's face was animated, his eyes gleaming brightly. Scobie had the feeling George Millson was thinking of his ex-wife at that moment, not Daphne Douglas.

Daphne's reaction after reading the letter had been a mixture of shock and uncertainty. Nowhere did Ruth Jones actually say the man was dead. But the passionate phrases and the underlying meaning, pointed to Max being implicated in his disappearance, if nothing worse.

Daphne looked at the date of the letter and the newspaper report. Why had Max kept them all these years? Forgotten? Not like Max. He was forever tidying his papers and discarding and weeding; it was almost an obsession with him. She read the newspaper report a second time. Perhaps Stanford Boley had turned up later safe and sound. Or perhaps not. She decided to find out.

It proved to be easier than she expected. She travelled down from London to the address given in the newspaper report and found Stanford Boley's mother still living there. Posing as a journalist, Daphne gave a false name and over a cup of tea she told Emily Boley she was researching old cases of missing persons for her newspaper. When a missing person turned up again—sometimes years later—papers often failed to report it, she explained. Usually because they didn't even know. Was that the case with Mrs Boley's son? Had he returned home or had she heard from him later?

No, Mrs Boley told her, he hadn't returned and she'd never heard from him, not a word. Had she any idea where he was going, the day he disappeared? Daphne asked. No, but Emily felt sure it had been somewhere not far away and if only she'd known where to look, she'd have searched for him herself.

As Daphne Douglas changed trains at Colchester North on her return journey to London, she was thoughtful. When she reached Liverpool Street an hour later, she'd taken a decision. She didn't care about Boley—it was clear from Ruth Jones's letter he was a dreadful man. Nor did she care what Max had been involved in thirty years ago, long before he married her. She only cared about today and keeping her husband.

Daphne tackled Max after dinner at their house in Wimbledon the day following her visit to Emily Boley. He was relaxing in an armchair with a brandy.

She stood at the cocktail cabinet, mixing herself a strong gin and tonic and studying Max's reflection in the mirror. He was a good-looking man and personable and charming. Despite his unfaithfulness and any skulduggery in his past, she wanted to hang on to him.

Turning round, she took a large mouthful of her drink and said quietly, 'You've been cheating on me, Max.'

He looked up. 'H'm? What, darling?'

'I've had you watched. A private detective has given me the sordid details—every damned time and place—so don't bother to deny it.' Her voice rose angrily. 'How *could* you humiliate me with all those girls!'

There was a moment or two of shocked surprise and then Max recovered himself. He was instantly contrite. 'I'm sorry, my dear, truly sorry. What can I say? These things happen, you know.'

'These things *happen*? Is that all you can say? You surely don't expect me to overlook this?'

'Darling . . .' His voice was caressing, his eyes smiling at her fondly. 'We get on well together. You're not going to let a few silly flirtations wreck everything, are you?'

'A few flirtations? Is that what you call them?' she snapped, her temper rising. 'Max, you've had a ball! This was adultery on a grand scale.'

'Those girls don't mean anything, Daphne, surely you know that?' he pleaded.

She looked away from the handsome, smiling face, determined not to be sweet-talked into accepting his excuses.

'Do you want a divorce?' he asked.

She rounded on him. 'You know damned well I don't!'

'Neither do I. Well, then . . .' He shrugged his shoulders.

Infuriated by his complacency, she said angrily, 'I won't put up with it! You've used my money all these years and this is the thanks I get. If you don't stop—stop completely —I'll call in every damned penny I put in your business. I'll bankrupt you. I'll cut you off at the knees, Max.'

He flinched as though she'd hit him and stared at her with a hurt expression on his face. She thought she'd won until he heaved a sigh and said, 'I can survive without your money if I have to, Daphne. So don't threaten me.'

She felt a sinking feeling in her stomach. She'd been sure that threat would bring him to heel. Now, she would have to try with this other business, see if that would pierce his smugness. Taking a breath, she said, 'I've made some other inquiries, Max.'

'What about?' His tone was relaxed, unconcerned.

'About the disappearance of a man called Boley.'

'*What?*'

His head jerked round like a marionette's. He recovered quickly, but not before Daphne had seen the naked fear in his face. She thrilled with a sudden exultation. Max was scared . . . and she'd never seen him scared before.

'What on earth are you talking about, Daphne?' he asked calmly.

Recklessly, she pressed on. 'His mother's still alive, you know. And his brother. I've spoken to them.' She saw the glint of fear in his eyes. 'They would like to know what happened to him.'

'Go on.' His voice was dangerously quiet.

'I found the press cutting about his disappearance and a letter from a girl in your deed box—and you needn't look so outraged. You've only yourself to blame. I would never have searched your private papers if you hadn't cheated on me. Boley did terrible things to this girl—a girl you loved —and it's obvious from her letter you were involved in his disappearance in some way.'

Max's expression changed, became earnest. 'The man was evil, Daphne, unbelievably evil. You don't know the half of it. He—'

'I don't want to hear about it!' she said sharply. 'I don't care what happened years ago before I married you. I only care about the present and saving my marriage.'

'I see.' He looked down into his brandy glass and swilled the drink around. 'Then what do you propose to do?' he asked cautiously.

Daphne smiled thinly. She had him in her power. 'That depends on you, my darling. And by the way, I've deposited Ruth's letter and the press cutting in my bank for safe-keeping. Everyone else may have forgotten about Stanford Boley, but I assure you his mother and brother haven't. Given the slightest hint, they'd go straight to the police.'

He stared at her in sudden comprehension. 'You don't mean you'd . . . ? Daphne, you wouldn't!'

'Oh yes I would,' she said grimly. 'Make no mistake about that. I wouldn't hesitate to tell them. You'd have the police here asking questions in no time. And I expect they'd find Ruth Jones and question her too.'

Max went pale. If the police got to Ruth . . . interrogated her . . .

Daphne's voice hardened as she delivered her ultimatum. 'I want my husband to myself, not shared with half a dozen floozies. These little flings of yours stop at once, Max, and you'll behave yourself from now on. Just one slip and I send Ruth's letter to Boley's mother.'

He sat in silence, staring down at the floor. The end of freedom, the end of his carefree love-life. Prison gates closing. He heard her voice soften slightly as she went on:

'And no more absences on business. I want you back in my bed of a night. You understand me, Max?'

He nodded. Not only incarceration, but forced passion with Daphne. The threat forever hanging over him that she could destroy him any time she chose. She had him strapped with that letter. He'd never be free again. By the time he'd finished another brandy Max Douglas had decided to kill Daphne.

He planned carefully. Over the following months, slowly and subtly, he won back her confidence. She was willing, even eager, to be convinced he still loved her and for a polished performer like Max that was no problem. He spent a year making sure everyone believed he and Daphne were a devoted couple so that, when it happened, no one would doubt for a moment her death was an accident.

At the end of the twelve months he checked her will to make sure she hadn't altered it and everything came to him.

And then he killed her.

CHAPTER 15

'Douglas lives here permanently now,' Scobie said as Millson brought the Sierra to a halt on the forecourt of Holly Cottage.

'How d'you know?' Millson asked.

'The secretary of the yacht club told me. Douglas sold his London house right after the funeral, along with this boat.'

'Lucky for some,' Millson said, casting envious eyes about him as they got out of the car and walked to the front door. He rang the doorbell and turned to admire the garden. 'When I retire, Norris, *I'm* going to have a cottage in the country. Not as grand as this, of course, not on my pension, but—'

The door behind them opened. He turned round and gaped at the youthful vision standing there. Max had told Poppy an old friend was calling to see them and he wanted her to look particularly nice. For the moment, while she decided what to do about marriage, Poppy was willing to indulge him. She was fully made-up and she'd had her hair re-styled. The silk suit she was wearing had a peplum and round her neck hung three or four long strands of beads.

'Er . . .' Millson closed his mouth. 'Is Mr Douglas in?'

'You must be Wilf.' Poppy held out her hand, playing the polite hostess. 'How d'you do? I'm Poppy Latimer, Mr Douglas's fiancée.' Her accent was pure Cheltenham Ladies' College.

Millson's mouth fell open again. So did Scobie's. Poppy dropped her hand and frowned prettily at the staring couple. 'Is something the matter?'

'Er—no. No.' Millson fumbled for his warrant card and showed it. 'I'm Detective Inspector Millson and this is

Detective-Sergeant Scobie. We'd like a word with your—
um . . . with Mr Douglas.'

'Oh, I see. How silly of me. Max is expecting an old
friend and I thought you were him. He's in the garden.
Won't you come in?'

Exuding charm and confidence, she showed them into
the sitting-room where they'd interviewed Douglas on their
last visit, six weeks ago.

'If you'll wait in here, I'll call him,' she said. 'Do sit
down.'

Millson puffed out his cheeks as the door closed. 'Fiancée!
And his wife less than two months dead. What d'you make
of that, Norris?'

'Perhaps they're not really engaged and she just said that
to explain her living with him.'

Millson glared at him. 'You mean that makes it better?'

'No, but she's quite a dish, isn't she?' Scobie said enthusiastically.

Millson looked down his nose. Poppy didn't seem much
older than his daughter Dena. 'She's far too young for him,'
he growled.

The door opened and Max Douglas entered, peeling off
gardening gloves. He was wearing olive green corduroys
and a pale green shirt.

'What can I do for you, Chief Inspector? Something more
about my wife's accident, is it?'

'In a way, sir, yes.'

Scobie noticed the 'sir'. Millson hardly ever graced anyone with a 'sir' and seldom out of respect. It usually sig-
nalled disapproval.

'I gather you're engaged to be married, Mr Douglas?'

'Yes. You've met Poppy. Enchanting, isn't she?'

'I suppose you've known the young lady some time? Since
before your wife's death, I mean.'

Max Douglas saw Scobie open his notebook and smiled
indulgently. 'You may find this hard to believe, Chief

Inspector, but I didn't meet Poppy until my wife's funeral. She was working at the florist's where I ordered the flowers. It was love at first sight.'

His smile expanded and Millson knew it had to be true. Not the 'love at first sight' nonsense, but the fact he hadn't met the girl until his wife's death. Douglas would expect them to check and he wouldn't have been that confident otherwise. Yet it had been months before her death when Daphne asked the inquiry agent to trace Poppy. Why had she kept the girl a secret from her husband?

Behind his confident smile, Max Douglas wondered what was the reason for this visit from the police. 'You haven't come here to congratulate me on my engagement, though, have you?' he prompted.

'No, sir, although that does have a bearing on things,' Millson said. 'When we spoke to you after your wife's accident you told us you and your wife were extremely happy together.'

'Yes, that's right. So we were. Doesn't mean I can't fall in love again. Some people say it's a compliment to the previous marriage when a man marries again.'

'Within weeks of his wife's death?' Millson couldn't help asking.

Douglas smiled tolerantly and Millson hated him for it. 'I do believe you're shocked, Chief Inspector. Is it the speed of our engagement or the difference in our ages that bothers you?'

'It's not my business to be bothered one way or the other about either, sir,' Millson said gruffly. 'What bothers me is why your wife engaged a private inquiry agent and had you followed—if your relationship was the happy one you described, that is.'

Max Douglas hid his surprise. So that was it. For some reason the police had continued their inquiries and unearthed Daphne's wretched private detective. That meant they hadn't been as satisfied about the accident as he'd thought. He changed his tolerant smile to an injured one.

'OK. I'm not denying I was a bad boy for a time. But that all ended a year ago when Daphne found out. We talked things over like sensible adults and decided to make a fresh start. The last twelve months were like a second honeymoon. Ask anyone who knew us, they'll tell you. As I said before, we were very, very happy.'

'I see, sir.' Max Douglas's continued insistence on his state of marital bliss didn't impress Millson, but he couldn't see a way to puncture it. He altered course.

'You say you didn't meet this girl until after your wife's death. Yet your wife knew her, apparently.'

Max guessed the inquiry agent had told them of Daphne's search for her former husband's lovechild. Now they were probably wondering if he'd murdered Daphne so as to be free to marry Poppy.

'Yes, that's right.' He glanced sideways at Scobie who sat with pencil poised. 'It's a little complicated, Sergeant. Poppy was the illegitimate daughter of my late wife's first husband—though no one knew about her when he died in a car accident. That's how I met Daphne, by the way. At his funeral.' He saw Millson's eyebrows rise. 'Her husband, Peter, was a distant cousin of mine. Which means Poppy and I are distantly related too . . . she's a third cousin once removed, I believe.'

'Why did your wife want to find her?' Scobie asked.

'She only learned of her existence last year. Poppy's father left her out of his will and Daphne thought the girl deserved something.'

'Yet she didn't mention this to you?'

'She didn't mention it to anybody, Chief Inspector. It was probably out of loyalty to Peter . . . she was trying to protect his memory, I suppose. It was Poppy who told me.'

Millson nodded and let a moment or two of silence elapse. In the break from taking notes, Scobie studied Max

Douglas. He looked completely at ease. Scobie's thoughts strayed to Poppy . . . wondering if she . . . His thoughts were interrupted by Millson shooting a sudden question at Max Douglas.

'Why was your wife making inquiries about a man called Boley a year ago?' Millson asked.

Max Douglas controlled his expression with an effort. How the devil had they got on to that? Fortunately, Daphne had told him what transpired between her and Emily Boley to reassure him she hadn't stirred things up and there would be no repercussions. How did the police know about it, though?

'That's an odd question. What on earth has this to do with my wife's accident?' he asked.

'Would you mind answering the question first, sir?'

'Oh, very well. There's no mystery. My wife wrote the occasional article for magazines and newspapers and she was thinking of submitting a piece about people who'd gone missing.' On a sudden inspiration he added, 'It was I who suggested the case of Sergeant Boley to her.'

Millson frowned. 'You *know* about that case?'

'Oh yes.'

'How come?' Millson asked.

'Well, it was in the papers. He was at Colchester Barracks when I was doing National Service there.'

Millson's nostrils twitched. There was a link between Boley and Max Douglas. While he was considering this, Scobie flipped back a page in his notebook.

'Mr Douglas, why did your wife tell Mrs Boley her name was Betty Smith?' Scobie asked.

Max had already worked out an answer to that. 'It was her pen name, Sergeant. She didn't write under her own name.'

'I see.' Scobie nodded. Douglas seemed to have an answer for everything.

Millson asked, 'You knew Sergeant Boley, then?'

'Yes. He was in charge of our training course.' Max smiled at Millson. 'He was a bit of a martinet.'

'Did he ever call to see you? After you'd left the army, I mean.'

'No. Why?' Max was becoming worried at these continuing questions about Boley.

'I'll come to that in a moment,' Millson said. 'Do you recall a night exercise at the end of your course?'

'Oh yes, indeed I do. Very well.' Max forced a laugh.

'Why was that?' Millson snapped, irritated by his light-hearted manner.

'Because I'd had a nasty accident the day before. I fell down an iron staircase and knocked myself out. I was in sick bay with concussion the night of the exercise.'

Millson hid his disappointment. If Douglas wasn't on the exercise he couldn't be the man who attacked Boley.

'So you didn't know Sergeant Boley was injured during the exercise?'

Careful now, Max thought. He'd been in an adjacent bed the other side of a partition when they brought Boley into sick bay two hours later, moaning with pain as he awaited transfer to a civilian hospital.

'No. No, I didn't,' he said. 'What happened?'

'Under cover of darkness someone made a vicious assault on him,' Millson said. 'And we believe that when Boley disappeared he was hunting the man who carried it out. That's why I asked if he called on you.'

'Well, now you know why he didn't,' Max said, with a superior smile. 'He'd know it couldn't have been me because I wasn't on the exercise, I was in sick bay. He could check from the sick records.' Max now felt sufficient confidence to ask the direct question. 'I'm curious, Chief Inspector. Why are you asking me these questions about Boley? It was all of thirty years ago when he disappeared and he's nothing to do with me.'

'Fresh evidence,' Millson said and saw dismay on

Douglas's face. On an impulse he said, 'Show him the notebook, Sergeant.'

This time there was a flare of panic in Douglas's eyes and Millson swiftly reached out to intercept Boley's notebook as Scobie went to hand it over.

'I said *show* him, Sergeant!' Millson said sharply, with a sideways wink at an astonished Scobie, 'not give it to him.' He took the notebook from Scobie and waved it at Max Douglas. 'Sergeant Boley's notebook,' he said. 'Hidden away in his mother's loft and just come to light.'

The bluff was working. Millson was certain that behind that stiff-lipped face Max Douglas was scared stiff of what might be in the notebook. There was a quiver at the side of the eyelids and the hands that had been lying relaxed along the arms of the chair were now clasped tightly together.

Millson hunched forward in his seat and tapped the notebook with his finger. In profile he reminded Scobie of a gorilla about to embrace its victim. 'Sergeant Boley wrote some names in here,' Millson said. 'Names of suspects. I believe one of these was the man responsible for his disappearance.'

He sat back, letting Douglas absorb his words . . . absorb the implication that his own name was written there. Douglas sat, rigid and still in his chair, unsmiling for once. There was no other reaction, however. The bluff had failed.

Defeated, Millson went on, 'We've been unable to find two of the men. A Corporal Tilley and a man called Mortimer. They'd have been at the barracks the same time as you. Do you remember them?'

The tension went out of Max Douglas. His name *wasn't* in that damned notebook, else they'd have said so.

'I don't remember anyone called Tilley. Mortimer . . . ?' He wrinkled his brow pretending to think. What should he say about Wilf? It was at Colchester they'd met and become friends. He didn't want the police talking to Wilfred Mortimer.

'Yes, I think I remember him. Only vaguely, though.'

Millson tried another ploy. He opened Boley's notebook and turned a page. 'There is one other name in here I have to ask you about, Mr Douglas.'

Max stiffened. God, what now? Had Boley written his name down after all?

Millson sat with the page open, deliberately letting the seconds pass, building tension.

'Yes?' Max asked at last, keeping his voice steady with difficulty. This villainous-looking policeman must have had ancestors in the Spanish Inquisition.

'Ruth Jones,' Millson said and watched the shock exploding in Max Douglas's eyes.

Ruth! Max struggled to quell the turmoil inside him. What else had Boley written in his notebook? With a supreme effort he managed to say calmly, 'The name means nothing to me.'

Max was certain no one had known about his affair with Ruth. Not even Boley, until he forced her to divulge his name. She'd been out with Wilf Mortimer several times and most people had thought *he* was her boyfriend.

'She was a WRAC in the RAMC . . . working in sick bay at the military hospital, I understand.' Millson looked at him expectantly.

'If we met, I don't remember her,' Max said.

'A clever blighter, Norris. He had an answer for everything.'

Outside Holly Cottage Millson punched the steering-wheel of his Sierra in frustration. Max Douglas had hustled them off with an apologetic: 'I'm expecting a guest, Chief Inspector, and I haven't even changed yet. So, if there are no more questions . . .'.

Millson glowered through his windscreen. 'I thought I

had him over the notebook. It knocked him sideways and he lost his cool for a bit.'

'But if he was in sick bay that night, he has an alibi for the attack on Boley,' Scobie pointed out. 'And if he didn't do that, then —'

'I'm still damned sure he killed his wife!' Millson said fiercely. 'I don't buy his story about her being a freelance writer. She'd have been more professional with Mrs Boley and she'd have been researching other cases besides Boley's. I believe Daphne Douglas discovered something and threatened her husband with it. And he had to kill her to silence her.'

Scobie couldn't resist asking, 'Isn't that *guessing* . . . sir?'

'A hypothesis, Norris. Not the same thing at all.'

Scobie kept a straight face. Sergeants guessed, chief inspectors hypothesized.

Millson started the car and drove out into the road. As he accelerated away, a car passed them and slowed to turn into the cottage. There was a middle-aged man in the driving seat.

'That'll be Douglas's friend, Wilf, I presume,' said Scobie.

Millson braked sharply, throwing them both forward in their seat-belts. 'Get the number, Norris!'

'Wha—?'

'The car that's just passed. Get the bloody number!'

'Right.' Scobie craned round in his seat and peered out of the rear window. 'Got it.' He pulled out his notebook and jotted it down.

'Wilf . . . short for Wilfred,' Millson said. 'Remember Eric Shand's last words? "Boley raped his girlfriend." Shand said: "*Wilfred* Mortimer." And Poppy said Douglas was expecting his old friend, "*Wilf*."'

'You mean the man in that car could be Mortimer, the fourth man?'

'It's possible. Check the Vehicle Owners index at PNC Hendon when we get back. If it *is* him, we'll have his address.'

CHAPTER 16

'You were right,' Scobie said in an awed tone as he entered Millson's office next morning. 'That car *is* owned by a Wilfred Mortimer. So it must have been him driving it. That was a bit of luck.'

Millson smirked. 'And a bit of quick thinking, Norris.' He rubbed his chin. 'Poppy Latimer said he was an old friend and Douglas told us he hadn't seen him since National Service days and only vaguely remembered him. Why did he lie?' He stood up and reached for his jacket. 'Where does Mortimer live?'

'Brentwood.'

'Right, let's go see him.'

'Mr Clissold will see you now, Miss Latimer.'

Poppy, in a white dress with pleated skirt and matching handbag and shoes, rose from her seat in the solicitor's office and followed the girl clerk along a corridor to a door covered with green baize. The girl tapped on the door, opened it and showed Poppy into Roderick Clissold's well-appointed office overlooking London's Bedford Square.

Yesterday, from a chance remark Max made to Wilfred Mortimer, Poppy had learned the name of Daphne Douglas's solicitors. Making the excuse she wanted to look round the West End shops for her trousseau, she'd come to London hoping Clissold & Clissold had been aware of Daphne's intentions about a trust fund and would be able to help her.

Roderick Clissold, in black jacket and striped trousers,

rose to greet her. He had a pale, intelligent face masked by heavy-framed spectacles and his dark hair was parted in the middle and brushed back. Giving Poppy a friendly smile, he shook her hand and waved her to a leather-upholstered armchair beside his desk.

He listened attentively, occasionally interposing a question, as she explained who she was and how Daphne had intended to pass on to her the inheritance her father had meant her to have.

'She said she was going to set up a trust fund and I thought—you being her solicitors—you'd probably know all about it,' Poppy concluded.

She felt a warm confidence in Roderick Clissold, inspired by the way he looked her in the face while she spoke. Not like that bald-headed lecher in Colchester who stared at her legs all the time.

He nodded. 'Yes, I remember Mrs Douglas did speak to me on the telephone about a trust fund. She was going to write to me giving the details, so that I could draft a deed for her approval. Next thing I heard, though, she'd had that tragic accident.'

'Oh.' Poppy's face fell. 'So, there was only a phone call?'

'I'm afraid so. Do you have any documentary evidence of Mrs Douglas's intentions? A letter, perhaps?'

'No, but I found a cheque stub that shows she made out a cheque to me for two thousand pounds.' Poppy opened her handbag. 'Here it is,' she said, handing it to him. 'I didn't receive the cheque and Mr Douglas said he couldn't find it.' She delved in her handbag again. 'And here's my birth certificate—you'll see my father's name is on it . . . and a copy of the family tree.' She pushed the documents across the desk.

'What does Mr Douglas say about the bequest?'

'He doesn't believe my father left a note with his will and Auntie D.'s father destroyed it. He says in any case I've no legal claim and my father should have put me in his will if he wanted me to have anything.' Poppy said angrily, 'It's not fair! He's practically a millionaire. He could easily let me have that money. He wouldn't even miss it. And it's mine really. He's stolen it from me.'

Roderick Clissold's tone was sympathetic. 'I understand how you feel, Miss Latimer, but, legally speaking, Mr Douglas is right. You have no claim. In fact, you would have had no claim at the time of your father's death either. Before 1975, an illegitimate child had no entitlement to a share of its father's estate.' He smiled wryly. 'Things are rather better today—but that's no help to you.'

Poppy heaved a big sigh. 'That's it, then. There's nothing else for it. I'll have to marry him.'

He was taken aback. 'I beg your pardon?'

'He wants to marry me. We're engaged.'

Roderick Clissold suppressed his astonishment and said politely, 'Congratulations.'

'Oh, stuff that!' she said rudely. 'What my father meant me have is worth an absolute fortune now and I can't think of any other way to hang on it.'

He goggled at her through his spectacles, shocked that she could tie herself to a loveless marriage to secure her inheritance as in some Victorian melodrama.

'You were my last hope,' Poppy said in a dismal voice. 'Can't you do *anything?*'

He stared at the three items she had placed on his desk: an old cheque-book; a birth certificate; and a family tree. If only he was a magician . . .

Mavis Mortimer answered the door. 'He's watching television,' she said in the tone of voice she might have said, 'He's biting his nails.' She turned her head. 'I'll call him.'

'Perhaps we could have a word with him inside,' Millson suggested as he realized she expected them to interview her husband on the doorstep.

'Oh, all right them,' she said grudgingly. 'Come in.' Preceding them down the hall, she shouted in a voice that made them jump, 'Wilf-RED!'

Scobie assumed her husband was watching television in an upstairs room, until a door at the end of the hall opened and a middle-aged man poked his head out. 'Yes, dear?'

'The police want you,' his wife said in an ominous voice.

'Really? What about?' He emerged into the hall, a tall angular man with thinning brown hair.

Millson pushed past Mrs Mortimer. 'I'm Detective Chief Inspector Millson and this is Detective-Sergeant Scobie,' he said. 'We're making inquiries about a missing person and we think you may be able to help us.'

'Who's missing?' Mavis demanded from behind him.

Millson turned, his bulk pressing against her in the narrow hall and causing her to shrink away from him. He disliked domineering, ill-tempered wives. He'd lived with one for ten years. He wasn't having this interfering woman present while he questioned her husband. 'It's *Mr* Mortimer I want to interview,' he said curtly.

Mavis sniffed. 'Oh, very well,' she said edging past him and making towards the kitchen door at the end of the hall.

'Perhaps they would like something to drink, dear,' Mortimer suggested.

'I'll get three cups of tea,' she said ungraciously, opening the door and closing it behind her.

Mortimer led the two policemen into the back room and switched off the television. 'Not much else to do,' he said apologetically. 'We're on short time 'cos of the recession.'

Millson nodded sympathetically. When they were seated he said, 'We're making inquiries about a man who disappeared a long time ago. A Sergeant Boley—or rather ex-sergeant. I believe you knew him.'

'Boley? Good heavens! Yes. That was ages ago. He disappeared, you say? When?'

'Back in 1961. Didn't any of your old army mates mention it to you?'

Mortimer shrugged. 'The only one I kept in touch with was a chap called Max Douglas and he obviously didn't know, else he'd have told me.'

Millson inclined his head and caught Scobie's eye. Clearly, Douglas hadn't told Mortimer of their visit either.

'Did Boley ever come to see you?' he asked. 'After you'd left the Service, I mean?'

'Funny you should ask that. Yes, he did. A couple of months later.'

'What did he want?'

'I'm not sure really.' Mortimer gave a nervous laugh. 'He asked a lot of questions about some exercise we did and then off he went. That was the last I heard of him.'

Scobie took out his notebook. 'Do you remember when that was, Mr Mortimer?'

'Let me see . . .' Mortimer screwed up his eyes. 'It was summer . . . July, I think. Sorry. I can't do better than that.'

'You're probably the last person to have seen him,' Millson said.

'Am I? Oh dear.' Mortimer looked worried.

Millson studied Mortimer's worried face and tried to imagine him as an angry young man, filled with passion and violence and exacting a terrible revenge on the man who assaulted his girlfriend. Later, murdering him perhaps. Millson's imagination refused to produce an image. Then logic took over and Millson reminded himself that angry young men often turned mild in middle age.

The door opened and Mavis Mortimer entered with a tray containing three cups of tea. On a plate were three biscuits. Millson waited until she'd distributed the cups and then resumed his questioning.

'I believe you went to see Mr Douglas yesterday?'

Mavis, half way to the door with the empty tray,

about-turned. 'I thought you went to Coggeshall yesterday!' she said sharply. 'What were you doing sneaking off
to see Max Douglas?'

Mortimer said apologetically to Millson, 'I'm afraid my
wife doesn't approve of Max.' He turned to his wife. 'I knew
you wouldn't want to come, dear. Max invited me over to
Duke's Green to meet Poppy.'

Mavis's eyes became saucers. 'You met . . . *her?*' She spat
the word.

'She's really very nice, Mavis.'

'Huh!' Mavis deposited the tray on the table, pushed the
door to and stood with her back against it. She addressed
George Millson. 'My friend Daphne—this man Douglas's
wife—was drowned two months ago. You know what he
did—right after the funeral? He took up with this young
trollop. It's disgusting. They're related, you know.'

'Mavis!' her husband said sharply. 'The Chief Inspector
isn't interested in tittle-tattle.' He turned to Millson.
'They're only very distantly related.'

Mavis snorted. 'Max Douglas and her great-grandfather
were cousins.'

Scobie was surprised to hear Millson ask, 'Would that
be first cousins, Mrs Mortimer?'

With a slight toss of the head at her husband, as though
to say, 'See, he *is* interested,' she said. 'Yes, that's right.'

Millson nodded and Scobie faithfully recorded the information in his notebook.

'Anyway, they're engaged to be married now, dear,'
Mortimer informed his wife.

'*Married?*' Her hand flew to her chest melodramatically.
'Ohh . . .' Her voice shuddered on a groan. 'How wicked!
Oh, how dare he! Poor Daphne!' She flung out her other arm,
a finger pointing at Millson. 'How would *your* wife feel if you
married a girl of eighteen right after you'd buried her?'

Scobie lowered his head to hide a smile. George Millson
was hardly the person to ask.

'I'm not married, madam,' Millson said solemnly.

'Oh,' said Mavis.

'Divorced,' he explained.

'Oh,' Mavis said again, in a different tone, her mouth turning down at the corners.

'I take it you know Mr Douglas quite well?' Millson said.

Mavis's lip curled. 'Not *him*. His wife, Daphne. She was too good for him, you know. He was one for the girls. Daphne brought him to heel, though. Had him over a barrel, she did,' Mavis declared with satisfaction.

'You didn't tell me about this, Mavis,' her husband complained.

'Why should I? Daphne told me in confidence. It was none of your business.'

'Did she have some sort of hold over him, then?' Millson asked with interest, wondering what else Daphne Douglas might have confided to Mavis.

Mavis's mouth closed like a trap. Scobie wondered if she was going to refuse to answer, like a priest guarding the confessional.

'Your information could be very important, Mrs Mortimer,' Millson said.

'Oh ... well ...' Mavis Mortimer's chest visibly swelled. She moved from the door and sat down at the table, looking around the room as though someone might be eavesdropping. 'Well ... Daphne found a letter from some girl. She didn't tell me what was in it, but she said she had Max where she wanted him. He'd never dare misbehave again, that's what she said.'

'Did she happen to mention who the girl was?' Millson's voice was casual, but Scobie noticed his eyelashes quivering like a girl's giving butterfly kisses.

'Ruth somebody ... common name,' Mavis said, screwing up her face in concentration. 'Jones! That was it, Ruth Jones.'

Millson let out a sigh. 'Thank you, Mrs Mortimer. You've been extremely helpful.'

Wilfred Mortimer was staring at his wife in disbelief. 'Ruth Jones? Mavis, are you sure?'

'Of course I'm sure!' she snapped.

Millson asked, 'Did you know Ruth Jones, Mr Mortimer?'

'Well . . . yes. We were . . . friends. It's news to me that Max knew her, though.'

'I might have known,' his wife said unpleasantly. 'You two together in the army . . . carrying on with every bit of skirt and—'

'It was before I met you,' Mortimer protested. 'And it wasn't like that. We—'

Millson interrupted them. 'When did Mrs Douglas tell you this, Mrs Mortimer?'

'Tell me what?' Mavis snapped, redirecting her wrath at Millson.

'That she'd found the letter.'

'About a year ago.'

'You drive, Norris. I want to think,' said Millson, opening the passenger door of the Sierra.

'Right. Where to?' Scobie asked.

'Marks Tey. See if Ruth Jones is home. If she's on duty we'll carry on to the hospital and interview her there.'

At the Anchor Garage in Tanniford, Lucas Boley wiped his hands on a rag and pulled off his mechanic's overalls.

Hunting through his office desk for an old VAT receipt that morning, he'd opened the drawer where he'd put the papers about his brother's medical discharge to hide them from his mother. The movement back and forth in the drawer had separated a printed leaflet from them which he hadn't noticed before. He picked it up. It was an old local

bus timetable with 'Valid to October 1961' stamped across
it.

Lucas unfolded it and saw that one of the routes from
Colchester had the times underlined in pencil and there
was a X against the stop in Duke's Green. *Duke's Green.*
Lucas gazed at the name with a puzzled frown, impulses
journeying the pathways in his brain. A connection was
made and his eyes narrowed. That was where the woman
who drowned had been staying. The woman who'd come
asking questions about Stan last year. Ma had shown him
the newspaper report: *wife of fifty-year-old Max Douglas . . .*
the right age to have served with Stan. Lucas Boley's eyes
gleamed. This was no coincidence. Stan had taken the bus
to Duke's Green. Douglas had a place at Duke's Green.
Douglas's wife had come asking questions about Stan.

Lucas had churned the knowledge around in his head for
an hour or two while he worked. The more he thought
about it, the more certain he became that Douglas was the
man his brother had been looking for. Lucas lifted the car
keys from a hook on the wall. He'd have the truth out of
this Douglas. Or else . . . Like his brother before him, Lucas
Boley believed in beating information out of people.

Clambering into his old Ford Capri, he drove up the hill
out of Tanniford and turned right past the Flag.

From the sitting-room window of Holly Cottage, Max
Douglas saw the white Ford Capri turn in and park on his
garage forecourt. A man in a black leather jacket heaved
himself from the driving seat. Max sucked in his breath.
Boley! With the police questioning fresh in his mind, Max's
eyes had deceived his brain and resurrected a ghost. He
shook his head and looked again. This man was in his
forties—too young for the real Boley and too old for his
ghost.

The image was so powerful, however, that Max went to
the hall cupboard, unlocked it and pulled his shotgun from

its retaining clips. Loading it, he returned to the sitting-room, placed it on the sofa and covered it with cushions.

The bell sounded on the front door. Squaring his shoulders, he went to the door and opened it. Close to, the likeness to Boley was even more striking. Max repressed a shiver.

'Yes?'

'Max Douglas?'

'Yes, who are you?'

'Lucas Boley. I wanna know what happened to me brother, Stan.'

CHAPTER 17

'If you'll wait in here, Sister Jones won't be a moment,' a nurse told them, showing Millson and Scobie into an uncarpeted room that was bare of furniture save for a small table and three chairs.

Millson lowered himself gingerly on to one of the chairs and pulled a packet of cigarettes from his pocket, then thought better of it and put them away again. He surveyed the cheerless room, his eyes coming to rest on a sinister-looking piece of equipment hanging on the wall with tubes attached to it.

'Enemy territory,' he said.

Scobie nodded. 'Like tackling a policeman in a police station.'

The door opened and Sister Jones entered, tall and authoritative in navy blue uniform, white starched cap high on her head. Millson realized his mistake in interviewing her at the hospital. This was her domain and he felt like a patient . . . ready to do as he was told . . . remove his clothes . . . lie down . . . submit to any indignity. Within these walls you were in their power. He supposed this was how the public felt on entering a police station.

He stood up automatically and so did Scobie. 'Please sit down,' she said. 'What did you want to see me about?'

Taking the chair at the table, she lifted a watch on a strap attached to her breast pocket and glanced at it. Every second vital, people desperately ill, needing her attention. Millson resisted an urge to apologize. This woman had lied to him, withheld important information.

'I won't keep you long, Sister.'

'Yes, I'm afraid I am rather busy,' she said.

'You didn't tell me you knew Max Douglas.'

Her eyes flashed briefly. 'You didn't ask me,' she retorted.

'Nor I did,' he admitted. 'So, I take it you do?'

'Not now. It was a long time ago.'

'Colchester Barracks in 1961?'

'Yes.'

'You were lovers.'

She flinched at the word. 'I don't see that that has anything to do with you.'

'This is a murder inquiry,' Millson said sharply. 'Answer the question, please.'

Her eyes widened slightly, but otherwise her face was impassive. 'Yes, we were lovers.'

'And Boley raped you. You lied to me about that.'

She swallowed. 'Yes.'

'And Douglas punished him for it.'

'I don't know.'

'Oh, come now—'

'I said I don't know,' she insisted.

Millson continued relentlessly, 'And afterwards Boley hunted him down and Douglas killed him.'

She shrugged her shoulders. 'I don't know that either.'

'I think you do. You wrote Mr Douglas a letter about it.'

She gasped and stared at him in shock. Slowly, she

sagged in her chair, her arms resting on the table and her head bowed. Millson waited. Outside in the corridor a trolley trundled by. Some poor devil on his way to the operating theatre, perhaps. She was the sister on a male surgical ward, he remembered.

Ruth Jones raised her head then stood up and walked to the window. She looked out. When she spoke, her voice was strained.

'Boley wanted Max's name and address. He beat me up. This is the hospital they brought me to.' She turned from the window. 'I was two months pregnant and I was hæmorrhaging.'

Her eyes roamed the sterile, clinical room, unseeing. 'Boley punched me with his fist—' she pressed a hand to her abdomen—'*here* . . . again and again.'

She moved forward and stood over Millson. 'He killed my baby! Max's child. *He killed it.*' Her lips peeled away from her teeth in an ugly expression. 'I hope he rots in hell!'

She turned to Scobie, her breast rising and falling with emotion. 'And you can write that in your notebook, Sergeant. Write it down. Sister Jones says . . .'

Her voice faded. Millson was on his feet just in time to catch her as she collapsed in his arms, sobbing.

'Why have you come to me?' Max Douglas asked Lucas Boley, keeping his voice level.

'Do me a favour.' Boley's mouth formed a sneer. 'You's the man me brother was looking for. An' he found you.'

Max wondered how much the man knew. More than the police, apparently. He adopted an air of unconcern. 'I'm afraid I don't understand. You'd better come in and explain.'

He showed Boley to the sitting-room, indicated an armchair and seated himself the other side of the room on the sofa, beside the hidden shotgun. Boley sat forward on the edge of the armchair, hands dangling over his knees. The likeness to his brother was extraordinary—same eyes, same thick lips and brutish face. Max had the eerie sensation it *was* that other Boley sitting there.

He listened to Lucas Boley's growling account of Daphne's visit to his mother and this morning's discovery of the bus timetable.

'Have you mentioned this to the police?' Max asked casually.

'Don't want no police. This is 'tween you an' me now.'

'This is absurd,' Max said. 'I don't know what you're talking about.'

'I know what you done to Stan. Ain't no use you denying it. I got all the facts, see?'

'You've made a mistake. I can prove—'

'Save your breath,' Boley growled. 'You's the guy Stan was after, all right.' The dangling hands clenched and unclenched ominously. 'He come here an' you's gonna tell me what happened.'

He stood up aggressively, his large hands hanging at his sides. Max eyed him nervously. The man was younger than he was and built like an ox. And vicious, like his brother. Max knew he would stand no chance against him in a fight. His hand dropped behind a cushion and grasped the stock of the shotgun.

'I'm gonna beat the truth outta you.' Boley moved forward, baring his teeth.

Max lifted the shotgun into view and Boley stopped. His eyes flicked over the gun and then he moved forward again.

Max pointed the weapon at his head. 'Stay where you are or I'll blow your head off!'

Boley halted.

'Get your hands up!' Max ordered.

Boley hesitated for a moment, then raised his hands.

'Now turn around and walk slowly out through the door.'

In the hall, Max lifted the heavy iron latch on the door to the cellar. Pulling it open, he reached inside and pressed the light switch. He motioned with the gun. 'Down there!'

Boley descended the steps to the cellar. Max shut the door on him and dropped the latch into place. He stood in the hall, thinking. Lucas Boley was a threat to the exciting new life Max was planning for himself with Poppy as his wife. He had to be disposed of.

Laying the gun on the hall table, he went out to the Capri. It was an old vehicle. Boley could easily meet with an accident driving along an unfamiliar road in this old banger.

Max went into the garage. Donning overalls and gloves, he collected a pair of spanners and wheeled a heavy duty hydraulic jack out on to the garage forecourt. Positioning it under the front axle of the Capri, he jacked up the car and crawled underneath with the spanners to slacken the nuts on the brake cables.

Lonely One Tree Hill at the top of the lane would be the ideal place for an accident. On the far side, the road fell away steeply to a sharp bend half way down. A runaway car, an old banger like this with sloppy brakes, could easily run off the road at the bend, crash through the flimsy wooden fence and end up down the old flint quarry there. He'd force whisky down Boley's throat to make him fuddled, drive the car up the hill, put him in the driving seat and send him off down the hill. To make sure of things, he'd loosen a nut on the fuel pipe so that if the crash didn't kill Lucas Boley, the fire that followed certainly would.

'She'd never give evidence against him,' Millson said gloomily as he and Scobie descended the hospital stairs. 'He's a knight in shining armour to her. She'd be a witness for the defence. But Douglas killed Boley—I'm sure of it now. And his wife.'

'Without a body, we don't have much evidence,' Scobie said.

'We have lies, Norris, big lies. We'll bring Douglas in for questioning. That should loosen his tongue a bit.'

In the cellar of Holly Cottage Boley examined his surroundings. There were no windows. The cellar was below ground and his only hope was the door. He went back up the steps and ran his hands over it. The door was smooth and solid and there was no way of raising the latch from the inside. Daylight showed between the edge of the door and the frame. He bent and applied his eye to the slit. If he could slip a lever of some kind between the door and the frame, he might be able to lift the latch.

Peering around in the light of the low-powered bulb, he saw some seed boxes stacked against the wall. He picked one up and ripped it apart, tearing a strip of thin wood from the side. Returning up the steps, he inserted the strip of wood between the door and the frame and slid it up to where the latch ran across the door on the outside. Levering upwards, he raised the latch from its seating and pushed open the door.

Stepping quietly into the hall, he saw the shotgun lying on the table. He picked it up and stepped cautiously into the sitting-room. Through the front windows he saw Max Douglas lying underneath the Capri with a spanner in his hand. Smiling grimly, Boley stepped back into the hall and out through the front door.

Max looked up and saw Boley standing over him with the shotgun.

'Tighten them brakes up again, else I'll blow you away!' Boley snarled.

'Yes. Yes, all right.' Max worked away with the spanners, then crawled from beneath the car and stood up. He pressed the release lever on the jack-handle. The jack folded with a hiss of air and the car sank to the ground.

'Wheel the jack into the garage,' Boley ordered.

Inside the garage he pointed to Max's Volvo Estate. 'Jack it up.'

'What for?'

'Do as you're told!' Boley raised the gun threateningly.

Max shrugged. Manœuvering the jack into position he jacked up the Volvo. 'Now what?'

'Get underneath the car and lie on your back.'

'Now wait a minute, I'm not—'

'Do it! Boley jabbed the barrel into his groin.

Max dropped to his knees and crawled beneath the Volvo. Boley looked down. 'You's not lying right. I wants your chest under the wheel and your crutch under the sump.' He prodded Max with the gun. 'Move!'

Lying on his back, Max watched fearfully as Boley took hold of the long jack-handle. He pumped it up and down, raising the jack to its fullest extent and lifting the front of the Volvo high off the ground. Resting his hand on the release lever, he gazed down at Max, an oafish smile on his face.

'Don't do to get under a jacked-up car with no support.' He gave an ugly laugh. 'The jack might fail. Now you's tell me straight what happened when Stan called on you. And don't give me no crap, else I drop this car on you and you's has a very nasty accident.'

'Yes. Yes, all right.'

Desperately, Max sought to justify himself. He told Lucas Boley he'd tried to reason with his brother the night he called, but his brother wouldn't listen. There'd been a fight and in the struggle his brother had fallen and struck his head on a marble table in the garden. Max could show Lucas the very table. It was still there. He was horrified to find the fall had killed Stanford Boley. He hadn't dared report it to the police because he was afraid they wouldn't believe it was an accident. But it was. Really it was.

Max ended his improvised tale and looked up anxiously at Lucas Boley. Would he accept this version of events?

Boley was chewing his thick lips, pondering Max's explanation. His hand was no longer resting on the jack-handle and he was holding the shotgun loosely with its butt resting on the ground.

Max was assessing his chances of rolling from under the car quicker than Boley could drop it on him or bring the gun to bear, when Boley suddenly asked:

'Where'd you put his body?'

'Does it matter?' Max pleaded.

'He has to have a proper grave. I wanna see it.'

Max hesitated, recalling the panic of that night. Wondering what to do with Boley's body . . . dragging it across the grass . . .

'*Tell me!*' Boley snarled.

Max told him.

'You bastard!' Boley's eyes blazed with anguished rage. His hand streaked to the jack-handle. There was a hiss of air . . . and the car dropped. Max's scream was cut off as the front wheel crushed his ribcage.

Lucas Boley hefted the shotgun in his hand and returned to the cottage. In the hall, he unloaded the gun and replaced it in the cupboard. Then, closing the front door behind him, he clambered into his car and drove away.

CHAPTER 18

Soon after Lucas Boley's Capri drove away, Poppy's red Mini purred along the lane, turned in to the cottage and came to a halt by the front door. Poppy, in a red skirt and red bolero jacket, red beret encapsulating golden curls, swung her legs from the car and stood up. As she made for the front door she noticed the open door of the garage and, wondering if Max had gone out, she changed direction to the garage to see if his car was there.

Putting her head round the door, she saw the rear of the Volvo and was about to turn away to the cottage, when she realized the car was standing oddly and sloping down at the front. She ran forward into the garage and saw Max lying beneath the offside wheel, white-faced and still.

She dropped to her knees and cradled his head on her lap. Suddenly his eyes flew open and she froze. The eyes were glazed and unseeing. Then, just as suddenly, the lids dropped over them again like a toy doll's.

Poppy stared down at the unconscious face. He'd had an accident, a bad accident, this man who'd cheated her. Her thoughts were in turmoil. This morning at the solicitors', Roderick Clissold had made an extraordinary discovery. She could scarcely believe it. And now, all at once, it was terribly important.

Her eyebrows came together in concentration. Max was helpless . . . arms pinned . . . at her mercy. Hardly breathing. She had only to lift her skirt . . . put it over his face . . . and her problem would be solved. Everyone would believe the accident had killed him.

As Millson's car approached Holly Cottage an ambulance emerged and drove away. Millson turned in and brought the Sierra to a halt. A police car stood at the front door, a PC leaning through the window speaking into the handset.

Millson jumped out, followed by Scobie. 'DCI Millson!' he snapped at the constable. 'What's happened?'

The PC straightened and saluted. 'An accident, sir. The young lady came home from shopping and found her—um —fiancé trapped under his car in the garage. Looks like he was adjusting the brakes when the jack gave way and the car fell on him. The ambulance has just taken him away.'

'Dead or alive?'

'Very much dead, I'd say, sir. We jacked the car up and got him out, but he wasn't breathing and there was no pulse. PC Wilson's inside the house taking a statement from the girl.'

'Any witnesses?'

'Apparently not, sir.'

'Right. Let's take a look.' Millson strode to the garage, followed by Scobie and the PC.

'That's our own jack the car's on now,' the PC explained as they stepped round to the front of the Volvo. 'The one we found under the car is over there.' He pointed to the hydraulic jack at the side of the garage. I thought forensic might want to examine it so we were careful how we handled it.'

Millson nodded. 'Good man. Now go and stop your colleague taking a statement from Miss Latimer and tell him not to ask her any questions. Then get on the radio and tell them I want a scene of crime officer up here pronto.'

'Very good, sir.' The constable hurried off.

Scobie stared at Millson. 'You don't think it was an accident?'

'No I don't, Norris. I believe the girl did it. I'm not sure how, but I mean to find out.'

Scobie gaped at him. Millson had taken leave of his senses—probably a reaction to the stress and worry over his daughter.

'For heaven's sake, George!' In his agitation Scobie made a rare use of Millson's first name. 'What possible motive could she have?'

'Money.'

'*Money?*'

'Yes. She cops the lot. Everything of his . . . everything his wife left him . . . the lot.'

'How d'you make that out?' Scobie asked.

'Mrs Mortimer said Poppy's great-grandfather was Douglas's cousin. Now, you remember Douglas told us Poppy's father was a distant cousin of his and he believed Poppy was a third cousin once-removed?'

'Yes.'

'She's not his third cousin once-removed. Douglas had it wrong. It's the other way round. She's his first cousin three times removed.'

Scobie looked blank. 'What difference does it make?'

'All the difference in the world, Norris. Douglas has no children, no brothers or sisters and his parents are dead. His wife died two months ago and I'm prepared to bet my pension he hasn't made a will since and he died intestate.'

'Doesn't that mean his money goes to the State?'

'No. Under the Intestacy Laws it passes to the next of kin in order of priority: children, parents, brothers and sisters, grandparents.'

'Then, Douglas doesn't have any next of kin—not living anyway.'

'Oh yes he does, Norris. His grandfather's the key. Mrs Mortimer gave us that.'

'But *he* can't be alive.'

'No, but if a member of one of the groups I listed is dead, their issue takes their place. Which means that Poppy Latimer, being a blood descendant of Max Douglas's grandfather, takes the grandfather's place and inherits.'

'Are you sure?'

'Absolutely. And so is she. You mark my words.'

Scobie's eyes filled with sudden suspicion. 'How come you know all this guff about intestacy?'

Millson's smile was shamefaced. 'I asked my solicitor when Douglas first told us about Poppy. I realized he didn't understand their relationship correctly and I wondered what she was up to.'

Scobie looked doubtful. 'Why get engaged to him?'

'To stop him marrying anyone else. She'd lose her inheritance if he did that and the best way to prevent it was to bag him for herself.'

Scobie frowned. 'But if they were married—'

'Ah no. She wasn't going to go through with it. The other

reason for becoming engaged was to get close to him. To give herself the opportunity to knock him off.'

Scobie said in a shocked voice, 'I can't believe that. She doesn't seem that kind of girl.'

'Don't be fooled by a pretty face, Norris.'

Millson saw the PC hovering in the doorway and waved him forward. 'Scene of crime officer is on his way, sir,' said the PC.

'Good. Now show me exactly how Mr Douglas was lying when you found him, Constable.'

The PC removed his cap and lay down on the concrete floor under the front axle of the Volvo, wriggling himself into position beneath the offside front wheel.

He looked up at Millson. 'He was on his back, sir, his head out beyond the bumper and his chest underneath the wheel with the weight of the car on him.'

'And the jack?'

'Folded down under the axle and just to his right.'

Millson stooped and gazed under the car. 'What was he doing, d'you think.'

'Adjusting his brakes, I'd say, sir. There's a couple of spanners on the floor here.'

'He'd be further under the car wouldn't he? Not lying under the wheel?'

'Perhaps he noticed the jack giving way and tried to get out.'

'Maybe. Thank you, Constable.' Millson straightened. 'Let's go and talk to Poppy Latimer,' he said to Scobie.

Poppy sat on the sofa in the sitting-room, the red beret and bolero jacket beside her. A PC perched awkwardly on an armchair, holding his cap. He jumped to his feet as Millson and Scobie entered.

Millson gave him a nod of dismissal and turned to Poppy. 'I understand you found Mr Douglas trapped under his car when you returned from shopping.'

'Yes, that's right.' Her voice was low.

'Where did you do your shopping? Colchester?'

'No. I went up to London for the day.'

'Was Mr Douglas alone in the house when you left this morning?' he asked Poppy.

'Yes.'

'Was he expecting any visitors?'

'Not so far as I know.'

'Did he usually do his own maintenance on his car?'

'I don't know. I haven't known him very long.'

'Yes, so he told us. You became engaged directly after his wife's death, I believe?'

Poppy's chin lifted. 'Not directly, no.'

'Within a matter of weeks, though.'

'Yes.'

'Was marriage his idea or yours?'

Poppy shrugged her shoulders. 'His, I guess.'

'It was what you wanted too?' Millson challenged.

Poppy met his eyes boldly. 'Yes. He's . . . was . . . a very attractive man.'

Scobie, disturbed at how Millson was spinning a web of guilt around Poppy and making her out to be a fortune-hunter, intervened to steer the questioning in another direction.

Ignoring Millson's angry glare, he asked, 'Did you see anyone hanging around the place when you came back?'

Her blue eyes turned towards him. 'No.'

'No sign of a car, for instance?'

She frowned slightly. 'Well, there was a car parked in the entrance to a field along the road from here.'

'Colour?'

'White, I think.'

'Make?'

'I only saw the back of it and I'm afraid I don't know much about cars,'

'Thank you,' Scobie said, satisfied he'd done something to counterbalance Millson's aggressive questions.

Millson gave him a disapproving look and came to his feet. 'I'd like you to come out to the garage, Miss Latimer, and show me exactly how you found Mr Douglas and what you did, please.'

Standing in front of the Volvo, Poppy portrayed the scene she'd encountered when she entered the garage. Millson listened carefully to her description of Max Douglas's position. It tallied with the constable's.

'Was he conscious?' Millson asked.

'No.'

'Was be breathing?'

She hesitated. 'I don't know. I—I think he was already dead.' He hadn't been, though.

'Did you touch anything? Try to jack the car up again, for instance?'

'No, I didn't know how.'

'So what did you do?'

'I ran to the phone and called the emergency services. Then I came back here and stayed with him . . . in case he came round.'

'And did he?'

'No.'

A man carrying a black box-like case appeared in the doorway of the garage. 'Take Miss Latimer indoors,' Millson told Scobie. 'I want a word with the scene of crime officer.'

As Scobie escorted Poppy from the garage, Millson beckoned the man forward. 'What's your name?'

'Hitchman, sir.'

'Right, Hitchman, see if you can get any prints off the handle of that jack.' Millson pointed to the hydraulic jack.

Hitchman nodded and laid the case on the bench. Opening it, he took out a pot of silver powder and a small brush. He dusted the jack-handle with powder, then took a puffer from the case and blew away the surplus. He peered at the handle.

'Some prints here all right.'

Millson watched him take a sheet of Cellophane from his case and cut a piece from it with scissors and carefully wrap it around the jack-handle, pressing lightly with his fingers.

'You'd better test those spanners as well,' Millson said, indicating the spanners on the floor. 'And see if you can find anything wrong with the mechanism of the jack. It's supposed to have given way.'

He walked out of the garage to the cottage and joined Scobie and Poppy in the sitting-room.

'D'you mind telling me *where* you went shopping, Miss Latimer?' he asked Poppy.

'Oxford Street,' she said. 'That's where I bought this outfit I'm wearing. In Debenhams.'

'Uh-huh. And do you know if Mr Douglas had made a will?'

'Yes.' She'd found it when she first searched the cottage. Roderick Clissold had asked her the same question. 'He left everything to his wife.'

Millson said sharply, 'His wife's dead.'

'Yes.'

Poppy wasn't going to say any more unless she had to. Roderick Clissold, gazing gloomily at the documents she'd laid on his desk, had picked up the copy of the family tree.

'Where did this come from?'

'Auntie D. gave it to me. It was my father's. She said I ought to know where I fitted into his family.'

He scanned it. 'Well, at least you don't have to worry about consanguinity.'

'You what?' said Poppy.

'Consanguinity . . . blood relationship. Your marriage won't transgress the Marriage Laws. You don't have to worry.'

'I wasn't,' she said.

'Half a minute,' Roderick Clissold said, still studying the document.

'Good God!' he exclaimed. 'Do you realize you're Mr Douglas's heir?'

'Getaway,' Poppy said, 'that's impossible.'

He seized a sheet of paper and began writing energetically, his pen flying across the paper. He finished writing and handed her what he'd written.

'*That* is a diagram of your exact relationship to Mr Douglas,' he said.

She stared at it.

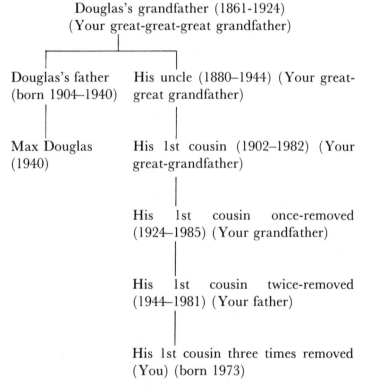

Douglas's grandfather (1861-1924)
(Your great-great-great grandfather)

Douglas's father (born 1904–1940)

His uncle (1880–1944) (Your great-great grandfather)

Max Douglas (1940)

His 1st cousin (1902–1982) (Your great-grandfather)

His 1st cousin once-removed (1924–1985) (Your grandfather)

His 1st cousin twice-removed (1944–1981) (Your father)

His 1st cousin three times removed (You) (born 1973)

Poppy looked up at him. 'You mean . . . if he died . . . ?'

He nodded. 'All other claimants are dead.'

She had been flabbergasted.

'So who inherits?' Millson asked, his eyes fixed on hers.

There was nothing for it. They'd find out anyway. Her chin lifted defiantly. 'I do,' she said.

'I *see*,' said Millson, as though he hadn't known already. 'Did Mr Douglas know that?'

'No.'

'You didn't tell him?'

'I didn't know myself until today when a solicitor explained it to me.'

Millson didn't believe her. 'What made you consult a solicitor?'

Better not tell him that, Poppy thought, it would only make him suspicious. 'It was a personal matter,' she said.

She had an idea he couldn't make her say and she hoped solicitors were like doctors and that Roderick Clissold couldn't be forced to say either. Anyway, Roderick would be able to handle the situation for her. He'd become very interested in handling her affairs when he discovered she was an heiress.

Millson didn't press her. There was time enough for that later. If she really had only found out today, then she was a fast worker. She'd taken the first opportunity—come home, found Max Douglas working under his car and killed him without a second's hesitation. Even Millson, hardened by years of dealing with violent crime, found that shocking.

Scobie, on the other hand, glancing at Poppy's golden curls and soft blue eyes, simply rejected the idea that she was the cold-hearted killer Millson believed her to be.

There was a tap on the door. Scobie stood up and opened it. 'The scene of crime officer has finished, sir,' he informed Millson.

'Good. Excuse us a moment,' Millson said to Poppy and went out with Scobie, pulling the door to behind him.

'Well?' he asked Hitchman.

'Nothing on the spanners. He was wearing gloves. I checked with the PC. And I can't find anything wrong with the jack. I'll have to take it away for the engineers to look at.'

'What about prints on the handle?'

John Hitchman opened his case and carefully took out a sheet of white paper to which he'd fastened the piece of transparent plastic. He laid it on the hall table. 'It's difficult because of the small diameter, but there's a good thumb and a finger, I think.'

'Right. I want you to take the girl's fingerprints.'

Millson turned and put his head into the sitting-room. 'This officer needs your fingerprints for the purposes of elimination, Miss Latimer. I take it you have no objection?'

'No.' She seemed unconcerned as she came out to the hall and watched Hitchman place two sheets of paper on the hall table and take out an ink pad.

When he'd finished she wiped her fingers on the paper towel he gave her.

'That's all for now,' Millson said. 'We're taking the jack away for examination. We'll be in touch with you again.'

She gave a faint smile and nodded. Scobie thought she looked relieved.

'All we need are her prints on that jack-handle and we've got her,' Millson said as they drove away. 'Motive . . . means . . . opportunity. And proof.' His expression was wolfish.

'I think you *want* her to be guilty,' Scobie said.

'She *is* guilty if there's nothing wrong with the jack and her prints match those on the handle. She said she didn't touch it.'

'If she's as cunning and wicked as you make her out to be, she won't have left her fingerprints,' Scobie retorted.

Millson looked annoyed. 'Killers make mistakes,' he said.

CHAPTER 19

In the backyard of their house in Tanniford next morning, Lucas Boley and his mother were enjoying the sun. Emily sat in a rocking-chair knitting, her face angled to catch the rays of warmth. Lucas lolled against the sill of the kitchen window. It was his day off.

'Tell me again 'bout the accident, Lukie,' said Emily.

She'd made him go over the story again and again since yesterday, never tiring of hearing it, and she knew it by heart, every little detail. How Lucas had forced Max Douglas to lie under his own jacked-up car while he questioned him about Stanford and satisfied himself Max was the man who'd murdered him. And how, while he was questioning him, the jack had accidentally slipped and the heavy car had fallen on Douglas, crushing his pelvis and chest.

'Did he suffer?' Emily asked, rocking rhythmically.

Oh yes, Max Douglas had suffered a lot, Lucas assured her. He'd taken a long time to die . . . very painfully.

'Don't s'pose you could do anything 'bout that, could you, Lukie?' She leered at him. They understood each other. She knew full well it had been no accident, but she enjoyed their game of pretence.

'That's right. I jus' stood there and watched him die, Ma. Jus' watched him die.'

Lucas painted her a harrowing picture of Max Douglas writhing in agony beneath the weight of the car and expiring very, very slowly. It wasn't true, but it made Ma happy and Luke Boley liked his Ma to be happy.

Smiling blissfully, Emily rocked her chair faster as she visualized the scene for the umpteenth time.

Millson's first phone call that morning was from the pathologist. Max Douglas had died from asphyxiation, consistent with his breathing being restricted by the weight of the car on his chest.

'Although, I'm surprised he didn't survive,' the pathologist said. 'He was in good health and his lungs were undamaged.'

'It was a heavy car,' Millson told him. 'A Volvo Estate.'

'Even so, I would have expected him to be able to draw at least some air into his lungs. Provided his intake wasn't restricted in some other way.'

'You mean by putting something over his face?'

'It was just a thought,' the pathologist said.

'Maybe it *was* an accident to start with,' Millson suggested when Scobie joined him for coffee. 'Let's suppose the jack failed and he was trapped under the car, but alive and breathing. She comes home—having just learned from her solicitor she stands to inherit a fortune—and finds Douglas in the garage . . . helpless. A ready-made accident victim. All she has to do is finish him off.'

Scobie put down his cup. 'You're making her into a real she-devil.'

'No, I'm speculating, Norris.'

A few minutes later there was a call from the engineers. They could find no fault with the hydraulic jack, it functioned perfectly.

'So, it was no accident,' Millson said. 'She saw him working under the car and seized her chance. Released the jack and dropped the car on him. Then smothered him when she found he was still breathing.'

'You're determined to nail her down in her coffin,' Scobie said gloomily.

'Just as soon as I have confirmation those are her prints on the jack-handle, Norris.'

*

John Hitchman, the scene of crime officer, phoned an hour later.

'Definitely not the girl's prints,' he told Millson.

'Damn!'

'A man's, from the size of the thumb. One other thing. Looking around yesterday, I noticed a recent patch of oil on the garage forecourt. It wasn't where the patrol car or the ambulance had stood, so I took a sample for analysis.'

'And?'

'It was sump oil . . . almost black. An old car, I'd say.'

'Thanks.' Millson put down the phone and called Scobie in from the next-door office.

'You'll be glad to know it wasn't your moppet's hand on the jack-handle, Norris. The prints were a man's and not Douglas's, he wore gloves.' He saw Scobie's smile. 'She must have had an accomplice,' Millson said, and saw the smile fade. 'There was another car at the scene earlier.'

'Poppy mentioned a white car,' Scobie reminded him.

'Yes, but she said it was parked along the road. And she wouldn't have told us about it if it was her accomplice's,' Millson said disparagingly.

'Why couldn't the car belong to someone else? Not an accomplice. Someone who was nothing to do with Poppy.'

'Who, Norris? No one else had a motive.'

'Lucas Boley.'

Millson pursed his lips, recalling the man's reaction to his brother's injuries, the murderous rage in his eyes. 'Possible. Does he own a white car?'

'Better than that,' Scobie said. 'While you were in the garage with Hitchman, I asked Poppy again about the car she saw. She drew it for me in my notebook.'

'That must have been nice for you,' Millson said.

Self-consciously, Scobie took out his notebook and showed Millson Poppy's drawing. 'I reckon it was a Ford Capri.'

Millson peered at the pencil outline. 'Looks more like an Astra to me.'

'No, it's a Capri.'

Millson sniffed. 'If you say so.'

'Luke Boley owns a Ford Capri.'

'How d'you know?'

'I phoned Kathy Benson.'

Millson glowered at him. 'Taking a bit upon yourself, weren't you? Why didn't you tell me this before?'

'I don't think you'd have listened while you were so set on Poppy as a murderess. But now we know those prints aren't hers . . .'

Millson nodded. 'OK. You've convinced me he's at least worth a visit.'

Poppy Latimer had had a busy morning. She'd phoned Roderick Clissold and he'd given her lots of advice and told her he would handle the formalities, she wasn't to worry about a thing. However, he needed Max's documents and papers and she'd been busily gathering them together. Added to that there were the household chores, instructions to the cleaning-woman, decisions to be made.

It had all come about so suddenly. Yesterday she'd been at her wits' end, undecided whether to marry Max or to cut and run. Today she was an heiress. It was a laugh. All she'd wanted was her rightful inheritance. Max had deprived her of it. And now he was dead she had everything. *Everything.*

She was worried about that horrible policeman, though. Not the nice sergeant with copper hair and blue eyes. The other one with cropped black hair, whose eyes went right through her. She was sure he hadn't believed her about Max being dead when she found him.

So easy, him lying there . . . arms pinned . . . to lift her skirt over his face . . . press down with her hands . . . She'd recoiled from the thought in horror. The very helplessness

that would have made it so easy cried out to her and she'd
jumped up and run from the garage to phone for help.

Then, minutes later, when she returned to comfort him,
he was dead. She couldn't understand it. His breathing had
been shallow . . . but regular. Yet it had stopped in the
brief time she was away.

She hadn't mentioned that to the police, though. They
might have suspected her of the very thing she'd shrunk
from doing.

Half a mile from Tanniford, in the bar of the Flag, Lucas
Boley ordered another drink. He was pleased the way he'd
fixed that scumbag, Douglas. Stan would have been proud
of him.

Lucas hadn't stood and watched Max Douglas die like
he'd told his Ma. That had been the trouble. Soon after he
drove away from the cottage, the consequences of his fit of
rage came home to him. Suppose Douglas wasn't dead, but
lying there injured? Able to babble accusations to the first
person who found him?

Lucas turned round and headed back, driving slowly past
the cottage to make sure no one had returned meanwhile.
It looked deserted still. He turned off the road into a gate-
way and hurried back to Holly Cottage on foot.

Stepping into the garage, he heard groaning. Douglas
was alive! Then, behind him, Lucas heard a car turn into
the cottage and scrunch to a halt. A door slammed and
footsteps came towards the garage. He dropped to the floor
and crawled under the rear of the Volvo.

There was the click-clack of heels on concrete and from
beneath the car he watched slim legs walk to the front of
the vehicle. The girl knelt, her skirt riding up to reveal an
expanse of thigh. Boley began crawling forward. If Douglas
opened his mouth . . . began talking . . . he'd have to top
the girl as well. Then suddenly she jumped up and ran out
screaming.

He scrambled from beneath the car and knelt beside his victim. With a hand under the head, he cupped the chin with the other and forced the mouth closed, forking his first and second fingers either side of the nose like a clothes-peg to clamp the nostrils shut. The head began to jerk spasmodically . . . Max Douglas's heels beat a brief tattoo on the concrete floor . . . and then he was dead.

Boley slipped from the rear door of the garage and along the side of a hedge to his car. To save turning round and driving up One Tree Hill, he drove on and took the lower road to Tanniford.

Lucas Boley was not at home when Millson and Scobie called at the house in Ferry Street. Millson started to explain to Emily that he could take the inquiries into her son's disappearance no further. He expected her to protest. Instead, she said amiably,

'Well . . . never mind. I's sure you's done your best.'

Surprised, he asked where Lucas was.

'Up the Flag, top of the hill, having a few drinks. It's his day off.'

'So he was working yesterday?'

'Not in the afternoon,' she said firmly. 'He was here with me, helping me pack.' That's what Lucas had asked her to say. 'He was here all afternoon,' she repeated emphatically.

'There are hundreds of Ford Capris and now his mum's given him an alibi,' Millson complained as he climbed into his car.

'She was very insistent about him being with her,' Scobie said.

'Too insistent.' Millson started the engine. 'Think that bird of yours is good for a coffee, Norris?'

'Not if you call her a bird, she isn't,' Scobie said sharply. 'She might be if you're polite. She might even be pleased to see you.'

'I'll put on my best behaviour,' Millson promised. He turned the car into East Street and up the High Street to the estate agent's. Kathy Benson looked up with a smile as he threw open the door.

'Just passing,' he said. 'Thought I'd drop in and see how my sergeant's best girl is doing.'

Kathy rose from her desk. 'How nice to see you again, Chief Inspector.'

'George . . . call me George,' he said cheerfully. He turned and peered out of the windows. 'I'll bet you see everyone who goes by here, don't you?'

'If I'm looking, yes.'

'Didn't happen to see Lucas Boley coming or going yesterday?'

'I did, as a matter of fact,' Kathy said.

Millson smirked at Scobie. 'When?'

Her auburn eyebrows came together. 'He drove out of the village at about four o'clock.'

'White Ford Capri?'

'Yes, that's his car. He came back just before we closed at six o'clock.'

'Thank you, Kathy. Come on, Norris. We have a man to see.'

'No time for a coffee?' Kathy asked.

'I'm afraid not,' Millson said.

At the car door Scobie said accusingly, 'That's the only reason you called on Kathy . . . to ask if she'd seen Boley.'

'No, I'd have stopped for coffee and a chat if she *hadn't* seen him,' Millson said.

At the Flag, Lucas Boley finished his drink and wiped his mouth with the back of his hand. Nodding to the barman, he went out to the car park. His Ford Capri emerged on to the road as Millson was parking his Sierra at the other end of the car park.

As the car gathered speed down the hill into Tanniford,

Lucas took his foot off the accelerator and transferred it to the brake pedal. There was no resistance. He stamped on it and the pedal went flat to the floor. Frantically, he pounded it with his foot.

Bucking and swaying, the Capri flew across the bridge over the railway, bounced off the brick parapet and careered across the road to hit the churchyard wall head-on. The force of the impact tore Lucas Boley's seat-belt from its mounting and catapulted him through the windscreen head first against the wall, smashing his skull like an eggshell.

Brake fluid had been seeping from the system since yesterday afternoon when Max Douglas had deliberately not tightened the nuts properly. Lucas had hardly used the brakes on his return journey to Tanniford, nor when he drove up the hill to the Flag.

When Lucas Boley's fingerprints were compared with those on the jack-handle, they matched. And an analysis of the sump oil in the Capri showed it to be the same as the oil found on the garage forecourt of Holly Cottage.

'I suppose it was just luck he caught Douglas working under his car in the garage?' Scobie commented.

'Either that or he forced him to lie down there while he jacked the car up and dropped it on him,' Millson said.

'Well anyway, that's three murders wrapped up.'

'Not completely, Norris. We only have two bodies. I wonder what Douglas did with Boley's.'

CHAPTER 20

A week after Max Douglas's funeral Poppy Latimer sold his Volvo and her red Mini and bought herself a silver Porsche. Shortly after that she sold Holly Cottage and rented a luxury penthouse in Knightsbridge. She hadn't intended to sell the cottage yet, but she was offered such a high price for it that Roderick Clissold said she'd be foolish to refuse.

Some months later, Kathy Benson learned who the purchaser was and told Norris Scobie.

Scobie found George Millson in his shirtsleeves when he entered his office. It was a hot June day and the room was full of smoke. Millson had given up his attempt to stop smoking when he heard his ex-wife had given up her custody case. Scobie had asked him why she'd called it off.

'Dena gave her an earful on the phone,' Millson explained. 'Let her know what she'd be in for if she made her go back. Very stroppy, she was.' He paused and looked thoughtful. 'You don't think she'll turn out like her mother, do you?' he asked anxiously.

'Not with you bringing her up,' Scobie had told him.

Scobie waved away some of the smoke. 'Emily Boley has bought Holly Cottage,' he said.

Millson stared at him open-mouthed for a moment, then reached for his jacket. 'I might have known.'

'Known what?'

'Come on. It's a nice day. We're going for a drive in the country.'

'I wonder where she got the money,' Millson said as he turned into Holly Cottage.

'Lucas Boley carried hefty life insurance. He wanted his mum to be comfortable if anything happened to him.'

There was no answer at the front door and they walked round to the rear of the cottage. Emily was in the garden, stooped over a bed of flowers with a trowel in her hand.

'Just passing, Mrs Boley,' Millson said. 'And saw you in the garden. How are you.'

'I's fine, Mr Millson, jus' fine.'

Millson looked down. There was a small wooden cross among the flowers.

'It's a Garden of Remembrance,' Emily said. 'In memory of my Stan.'

She put down the trowel. 'I'll go and put the kettle on. You'll stay for a cup of tea, won't you?' She shuffled away to the back door.

Scobie gazed at the rectangular border of small shrubs surrounding the flowers. 'Looks a bit like a grave,' he said.

'It *is* a grave,' Millson said. 'That's where Boley's body is buried.'

Scobie gaped at him. 'How d'you know?'

'Deduction, Norris. This is where Douglas lived in 1961 and so it's where the confrontation took place. I couldn't understand why Mrs Boley suddenly lost interest in her son's disappearance. It was because Lucas dragged the truth from Douglas before he killed him, including where he'd hidden his brother's body. He told his mum and that's why she bought the cottage. Because Lucas told her Stan's body was here.'

Millson waved a hand. 'He's right there . . . under those flowers. Not that we can do anything about it.'

Millson wasn't quite correct. Boley's body wasn't buried beneath the flowers. It wasn't buried at all. After murdering him that night thirty years ago, Max Douglas had dragged the body across the grass to the only place he could think of to hide it—the old septic tank, disused since the cottage had been put on main drainage.

Lucas had told his Ma that Stan was buried beside the concreted-over manhole cover. He didn't tell her he was lying in the sewage in the tank below. Ma wouldn't have liked that.